CELG

EMBRACEABLE YOU

Chrissy Grieves is good at her job at McGregor's Transport, and works hard — which leaves her little time for relationships. Besides, she's been unlucky in love, and her mother hasn't exactly been the best role model in that department. So when the boss's son, Mark, is brought home to keep an eye on the business while his parents are on holiday, the last thing Chrissy expects is to fall for him — and she's determined to keep her distance. Can Mark persuade her to take a chance on love?

SUZANNE ROSS JONES

♦

EMBRACEABLE YOU

Complete and Unabridged

LINFORD
Leicester

First published in Great Britain in 2016

First Linford Edition
published 2016

A catalogue record for this book is available
from the British Library.

ISBN 978-1-4448-2838-2

Published by
F. A. Thorpe (Publishing)
Anstey, Leicestershire

Set by Words & Graphics Ltd.
Anstey, Leicestershire
Printed and bound in Great Britain by
T. J. International Ltd., Padstow, Cornwall

This book is printed on acid-free paper

1

A Request

Mindful of dogs, cats, and chickens, who were all apt to roam, Mark McGregor slowed his car to a crawl as he drove into the farmyard. He wasn't looking forward to the next hour or so. There had been something in the tone of his mother's voice when she'd phoned to tell him about this family meeting — something that hinted he wasn't going to like what his parents had to say.

'Has Dad had a relapse?' he'd asked, giving voice to his greatest fear. Since their father's recent heart attack, Mark and his two brothers had naturally been concerned about their parent's health.

'No, it's nothing like that,' she'd assured him. But she'd refused to give him even a hint of what this was all about.

The deafening blast of a vehicle's horn somewhere close behind his car had Mark nearly jumping out of his skin. 'Hurry up and park that thing,' an angry voice shouted. An angry female voice. 'Some of us have schedules to keep to.'

A glance in his rear-view mirror confirmed his suspicion: It was Chrissy, head peeking out of the window of a large lorry, long red hair pulled into a ponytail.

He grinned. Some things never change, and Chrissy Grieves — McGregor Transport's office manager — being impatient to get things done was one of those. He lifted his hand in acknowledgement, and drove his car into the space between his older brother Jack's estate car and younger brother Ryan's four-wheel drive.

Chrissy had already parked her truck by the time Mark was out. She didn't look too happy as she marched past towards the house.

'Hey, wait up,' he called after her, taking several long strides in her direction as two lively collies followed in his wake.

There was no mistaking her reluctance as she waited for him. Her hands were firmly planted on the hips of her faded denim jeans, and she made no move to return his smile. He'd never quite been able to get over the feeling that she didn't like him — and he couldn't work out why.

'What's the matter?' he asked.

'It's like I said — I'm pushed for time. There are two drivers off sick today and I still haven't started the admin.'

She worked too hard. They all knew it. As well as managing the office and the staff on a day-to-day basis, since Denny McGregor's illness she'd also taken up the slack when an extra driver was needed.

'Is there anything I can do to help?'

Her expression softened, even if it wasn't quite into a smile, and she shook her head. 'I've done the urgent delivery and I'll stay late to get the wages done.'

They walked into the house together, and Mark wondered what McGregor Transport would do without her. They all knew she effectively ran things these days — with only the occasional input from the eldest of the brothers, Jack. She'd said that she was happy to do it; but as he looked down at her pale, frowning face now, he did wonder if perhaps it was too much to ask. Maybe the three brothers should have been a bit more insistent on helping out.

'Why are you looking at me like that?' she asked, meeting his gaze with huge green eyes as they stopped by the door. She really was extraordinarily pretty. He'd always known it, of course — but he'd never been the type to make a nuisance of himself with women who didn't reciprocate his interest.

'You work too hard,' he said as he opened the door and allowed her to pre-cede him into the McGregor farmhouse. When she grinned he saw she wasn't just pretty, she was beautiful; and, quite unexpectedly, his breath caught.

'Someone's got to get it all done,' she said over her shoulder as she walked away.

He watched her progress down the hallway, knowing he shouldn't. It seemed wrong somehow to dwell on the gentle sway of her denim-clad hips and the swinging of her fiery red ponytail. It was only when she'd disappeared through the door to the office, though, that he went to join the family meeting taking place in the kitchen.

The family — mother, father, and his two brothers — were already seated around the scrubbed wooden table. Heather McGregor was on her feet as soon as he stepped into the room.

'Cup of tea?' she asked.

'Thanks, Ma — but sit down, I'll get it.'

He smiled as she waved him to a seat and headed for the kettle. She cut him a generous slice of chocolate fudge cake while she was on her feet, without asking. But that was nothing out of the ordinary. Nobody ever went hungry or thirsty in this house.

'OK, boys,' Denny started once everyone was settled, 'your mother and I asked you here today because we've got something quite serious to discuss.'

Heather bit her lip and nodded in agreement.

Mark glanced around at his brothers. Their frowns mirrored his own. It was pretty obvious from their expressions that they shared his concern.

'You all know your father hasn't been well.' Heather looked at each of her sons in turn. They all nodded. 'Well, the doctor's suggested he take things easy for a while.'

Youngest brother Ryan sat up in his chair. 'What exactly did the doctor say?' he demanded. As a nurse, he was keen for all the medical facts.

Heather patted Ryan's hand. 'Nothing to worry about. He just thinks, as I do, that it would do your father good to stay away from work a little longer. Isn't that right, Denny?'

Denny McGregor mumbled something

incoherent and didn't look too pleased about it.

'We've decided,' Heather continued, 'that the only way your father will be able to take a proper break from the business is if we go away. So I've booked us on a month-long cruise of the Mediterranean.'

There was silence as the three brothers absorbed this news. Their parents hadn't been away on holiday in living memory. What was more, they had a history of trying to shield their sons from worrying truths. When the haulage company had been in trouble a short while ago, it had taken months for them to come clean.

Mark was sure he wasn't alone in wondering if there was more to this announcement.

Heather glanced from one son to the other and, when none of them spoke, she carried on. 'We need to decide now what we're going to do about the business while we're away.'

Denny nodded. 'Chrissy's capable

and dedicated,' he said, finally finding his voice, 'but you all know we can't take advantage of her work ethic. So we need to find other hands I trust — McGregor hands. I need one of you boys to look after things for me for a few weeks.'

2

Stepping Up

For a few moments, the three brothers sat in silence and absorbed this information. And all Mark could think of was that things must be bad if his father was stepping away from work. He loved his business; had built it up from nothing. He wouldn't be taking a break unless there were serious issues with his health.

'Is there something you're not telling us?' Eldest brother Jack was the first to voice what they'd all been thinking.

Denny shifted in his chair under Jack's careful scrutiny. But his blue eyes were unflinching as he met his son's gaze. 'It's as your mother says, son. I need to take a break from work, and I won't be able to do that if I'm at home. So she's put her foot down and is taking me on a holiday.'

'Are you sure, Dad? The doctor didn't give you bad news, did he?' Mark asked.

'No, he didn't.' Denny McGregor smiled and looked around at his three boys. 'But we do still have the problem of leaving the business: Will any of you be able to hold the fort for a month? You'd only need to oversee things and be here in case something goes wrong. Chrissy will keep everything in order like she always does.'

'I'll do what I can,' Jack promised.

'And you'll move in here to keep a proper eye on things?' Heather asked hopefully. 'That's the only way your dad will relax — if he knows one of our boys is taking care of things at home.'

Jack ran impatient fingers through his hair. 'Moving in would be a bit difficult. If it was just me, then of course I'd do it, but I've got Paula and Jess to think about.'

'Can you talk to them?' Heather asked anxiously. 'Ask them if they'd be willing to move here, too? If you explain, I'm sure they'll agree.'

'It's not quite that simple. Jess has exams coming up at school and could do without the disruption.' Jack paused to look at the faces around the table. 'And Paula . . . well, Paula and I had hoped to both tell you together, but we've just found out we're expecting a baby.'

Heather was on her feet in an instant. 'Oh, how wonderful.' She hugged her eldest boy. The others added their congratulations and hearty handshakes and back slaps were exchanged.

'I don't see how that stops you all moving to the farmhouse,' Ryan said.

'Paula's having a tough time of it with morning sickness,' Jack confided. 'So I've been opening the café for her and doing the breakfast shift. It would mean leaving her even earlier if we lived up here.'

It would only be a few minutes earlier, Mark knew, but it was under-standable, under the circumstances.

11

Jack wouldn't want to leave his wife on her own for even a moment longer than was necessary, especially when their house in the village was only a short walk across the street from the café. While Jack was serving breakfasts, he would be on hand should Paula need him.

'She's going to kill me for letting the cat out of the bag,' Jack added with a sheepish grin. 'She was so excited about making an announcement.'

'Paula's an angel,' Heather declared, obviously unwilling to hear a word against her daughter-in-law, even if it was a light-hearted word. 'She'll forgive you when she realises we pushed you into a corner.' Jack nodded.

'Does Jess know yet?' Heather asked, mentioning Jack's daughter from his first marriage.

'She guessed when Paula was sick every morning.'

Heather laughed. 'That's teenage girls for you.'

'She's delighted,' Jack added. 'Already counting up the extra pocket money she'll earn from babysitting.'

Everyone laughed, but all too soon Denny's smile faded and it was time to talk business again. 'Will one of you two be able to help?' He looked between Ryan and Mark. And their smiles dimmed, too, as the brothers looked at each the other.

'I don't see why I can't carry on doing what I've been doing since you were in hospital,' Jack appealed to his father. 'It's worked really well up until now with you taking a back seat. Chrissy knows she can phone me if there's a problem — and I can drop in a bit more often.'

But Denny McGregor shook his head. 'It wouldn't be fair on Chrissy,' he said quite reasonably. 'Besides, she's never been completely alone. You mother was here as backup when she wasn't visiting me — and Mark was staying, too.'

'It would be too much for Chrissy,' Mark added quietly, and all eyes turned to him. 'I saw her when I arrived; she's rushed off her feet and talking about staying late to catch up on the paper-work.'

They were all thoughtful for a moment.

'We definitely need someone to stay here,' Heather added. She glanced across to where Tibby, an elderly cat, slept near the Aga. 'Apart from Chrissy needing backup, someone has to look after the animals.'

They might rent most of their land out to a neighbouring farmer, but Denny and Heather McGregor still kept a number of animals at the farmhouse. As well as the cat and the two border collies, there were hens and an elderly donkey. Mark realised it would be impossible to farm them all out. And Chrissy already had too much to do without having to worry about her employers' pets. His parents were right — the only solution was for someone to stay here.

'And with all the lorries on the premises,' Denny added, 'we can't leave the place unattended overnight.'

Heather turned towards her youngest

son. 'I suppose your shifts at the hospital would rule you out, Ryan?'

Ryan sighed. 'I'd love to help,' he said. 'But I can't promise to be here overnight when I'm on a late shift.'

They all nodded. 'Of course not.' Heather patted his arm.

And, suddenly, all eyes were turned towards Mark.

'I have to get ready for my exhibition,' he said, hating that he wasn't jumping at the chance to help his parents. 'I've still got a number of canvasses to finish and not much time left.' But it was more thinking out loud — trying to find a way around the problem rather than an out-and-out refusal. He might have a purpose-built studio at his own home, but of the three brothers, he was the most flexible in terms of being able to please himself.

And, of course, there was Chrissy. Even if she did hiss and spit when she saw him, there was something undeniably appealing about being the one she might turn to if she needed help with running the transport business.

'You'd be able to paint here,' his mother told him, coaxing him when she obviously didn't realise that his mind was already made up. 'The new barn's empty and would be perfect for you to work on your larger canvasses.'

The barn: his mother had suggested he work there when he'd stayed with her while his father had been in hospital. He hadn't been able to tell her then that the vibes, not to mention the lighting and security, were wrong — and he couldn't bring himself to tell her now.

He would work his way around it somehow. It should be easy enough to fit an alarm. And maybe if he threw the doors wide open, he would have enough natural light to work by during the day. He'd bring in some lamps, too, for when he'd have to work late. But, really, how much help would he be? He had no business experience. He couldn't even drive any of the lorries.

His father looked pointedly at him. 'I'd appreciate it if you could help, lad.

16

I know you've got your painting, but that's something you could get away from a lot easier than your brothers can get away from their jobs.'

Mark tried not to smile at his father's words. Denny and Heather had never taken their middle son's career seriously. They viewed his painting as a hobby — something he might earn a little pocket money with; something he might one day grow out of, at which point he'd be able to get a proper job. He couldn't blame them. He knew they were both practical people who had both run businesses with a tangible purpose. It was difficult for them to see, he knew, how much of himself he put into his art. But, compared with structural engineering and saving lives, he knew his parents saw his work as frivolous.

'Dad, Mark has an exhibition soon,' Ryan said. 'He'll be tied up with that.'

'But he can paint his pictures here,' Heather said again.

'He has a state-of-the-art studio at his house. It would be difficult for him to leave that and to bring his work down here,' Jack said.

'But it's not like a proper job,' Denny persisted.

This time, Mark couldn't prevent a smile. He knew he should be offended, but his parents weren't being unkind — they didn't understand, that was all. And that was probably his fault, because he didn't talk about his work to them.

'Mark earns more from one of his paintings than I do in a year,' Jack told his father wryly. 'He's as highly regarded in his field as I am in mine — or Ryan is at the hospital. I'm sure, between the three of us, we can work something out.'

Mark was grateful to his brother for sticking up for him, but he accepted there was no other choice. 'When would I need to move in?' he asked.

His mother's smile was hopeful. 'As soon as possible. We're leaving next week. I want to get your dad away before he changes his mind.'

Mark nodded. 'OK,' he said. 'I'll

move in to keep an eye on things here while you're away.'

His parents' smiles were all the reward he needed. He mentally kicked himself that his fears of being unqualified for the role had meant he hadn't leapt at the chance to help out. After all, they only needed someone to babysit the animals and to keep an eye on the lorries.

'Thank you, son.' Denny McGregor slapped him on the back.

'Don't thank me until you see what a mess I make of the place,' Mark said with a self-conscious laugh. 'I'll be clueless if Chrissy needs help.'

Heather shook her head. 'My boys can do anything they turn their minds to,' she said with confidence Mark wished he could share. He hoped, if Chrissy allowed him and he had time between working on his paintings, he could learn to help out with the business; take some of the pressure from her.

Ah — that was one thing they hadn't factored into this equation. It was well known Chrissy wasn't fond of having her routine disrupted, or of having her authority questioned. She wasn't going to be happy to have a new McGregor in charge. Particularly not when Mark was the McGregor in question.

She'd grown up around the brothers; been almost a part of the family. When she was a child, her father had been a valuable member of staff, and she'd accompanied him to work every chance she got. But she'd never been as easy in Mark's company as she had been in Jack's and Ryan's. She could laugh and joke with those two all day, but Mark knew she was always guarded around him. He'd always suspected she didn't like him much, though he'd never discovered why. Judging by her reaction to him earlier, he further deduced she must still feel the same way, as she hadn't been able to get away from him fast enough.

'Just one thing,' Mark said, and they all turned expectant eyes towards him. 'Who's going to tell Chrissy?'

3

Telling Chrissy

Chrissy was finding it difficult to concentrate. She shuffled papers noisily on her desk and tried once more to get on with her work. She knew what had unsettled her. It was him — Mark. Of the three McGregor brothers, he was the one she found hardest to fathom. He was quiet — too quiet. Not outgoing like the other two. You never knew what Mark was thinking. Heather had always said he was deep.

Chrissy sighed as the figures refused to add up yet again. 'Get a grip,' she told herself sternly. She wanted to be able to go home at some point today, but the way things were going she'd be here all night.

She needed to concentrate on her work and forget all about Mark

McGregor. She couldn't believe she was allowing him to disrupt her thought processes like this. All they'd done was exchange a few words. But there had been a moment when he'd looked at her earlier that she'd fancied . . .

No. She shook her head. She wasn't Mark's type — and he wasn't hers. Definitely not.

'Hi, Chrissy.'

Her head snapped around and she found Mark standing in the doorway, almost as though she'd conjured him up just by thinking of him.

'What are you doing there?' she asked, trying to keep her tone light. Though she suspected, from the clenching of his jaw, that she'd sounded sharp. She wondered if she should apologise. It wasn't his fault she was always unsettled around him.

'I need to talk to you.' Before she could say anything, he'd stepped in to the office and had pulled up a chair and was sitting across the desk from her. His expression was serious, and Chrissy felt her stomach churn. Whatever he had to say, she was pretty sure she wasn't going to like it.

She'd known something was up when she'd driven into the yard and found all three McGregor boys' cars there. She should have followed her instinct and asked Mark straight out when they'd walked into the house together. Or else asked to speak directly to Denny and Heather.

'What do you want to talk about?' she prompted when he didn't speak.

He looked at her, his blue eyes unfathomable. He seemed to be weighing up the situation; weighing *her* up. And she wanted to tell him to get a move on; he knew she was busy. He had no business wasting her time like this.

He raked a hand through his red hair, making it stand on end in a fashion she reluctantly found endearing. 'You know Dad hasn't been too well?' he asked quietly.

She gave a little gasp. Oh, that didn't sound good. She immediately felt horribly selfish. Here she was worrying about herself, when it seemed there were further problems with Denny's health. 'Is he going to be OK?'

Mark nodded. 'So he says. But the doctor's warned him he needs to take a complete rest while he recuperates properly.'

She sighed with relief. Heather and Denny McGregor were the best employers in the world. They treated her more like one of the family than an employee. The thought of something happening to either of them was unbearable. 'I'll do what I can here so he doesn't need to worry.'

'I know you will,' he said. 'We all know how much you've done already, and the family's very grateful. But Mum's decided to take him away completely — on a Mediterranean cruise.'

'Oh.' That was a complete surprise. She knew how much the McGregors loved this place; they hardly ever even went for even a weekend away. It had to be serious if Heather was taking her husband on a proper holiday.

'They're worried about leaving the place for that time, though.'

That figured. 'I'll manage things here,' she rushed to tell him. 'I've been running the business more or less since your dad was taken ill in any case.'

'I know that. But the thing is, they want me to move in.'

It was none of her business. It wasn't as though she lived here. Even if he did move in, she could still do her job, and then at the end of the day go home and forget all about Mark McGregor. But, even while she told herself that it shouldn't bother her, it did. She shifted in her chair as she thought through the implications. He'd be here when she arrived in the mornings. He'd be here when she telephoned clients. Or did the wages. Or the books. And he'd be here when she came back from deliveries. And when she was giving the drivers their orders. That knowledge disturbed her almost as much as his silent scrutiny was doing just now. His gaze burned into her — and it unnerved her. Though she was determined not to let him see.

'I'm perfectly capable of running this place on my own,' she told him, refusing to drop her gaze as she attempted to stare him out. 'I think I've proved that over the past months.'

'Nobody doubts you could cope alone, Chrissy,' he told her quietly, his voice sending unwelcome shivers down her spine. 'And you will be given a free hand with the business, as you've been used to these past weeks. But . . . '

'But what?' she demanded, feeling angry heat on her cheeks.

'But there are the animals, security overnight . . . As a family, we can't ask you to take charge of all that. It wouldn't be fair. And one of us should be on hand, just in case it all becomes too much.'

'It won't.'

'You're already overworked,' he reminded her.

'I can cope. And I can easily deal with the animals, too.' What was there to do? Feed them, occasionally talk to them — as she already did in any case. And close the hens in at the end of the day to keep them safe from foxes. She could so do that. There was no need for this big, disturbing man to disrupt everyone's routines, including his own, by moving in here.

Although she didn't actually tell him what was on her mind, something must have shown in her expression, because he sighed. 'I won't interfere,' he promised. 'Not unless you ask for my help. I'll have my own work to be getting on with.'

'Painting.' She was shocked at how annoyed she sounded; the implications he might take from her tone. She was worried she might have offended him. An apology was ready on her tongue. But he smiled — disarming her so completely that she felt her mouth form a silent 'Oh' and she blushed even hotter.

'Yes,' he agreed easily. 'Painting. I have a deadline — and an exhibition to prepare for, so I won't have time to get involved. Unless . . . ' He smiled, turning her insides to jelly. 'Unless, that is, you need me.'

That disturbed her more than anything — the thought she might need Mark. 'Then why move in here? I can phone you if there's a problem.' Or, more likely, she'd phone Jack or Ryan.

'Dad asked me to,' he said simply.

And that was when Chrissy knew she'd lost the fight. Because, however much she didn't like the thought of the very disturbing Mark McGregor being in residence at the farmhouse, she wouldn't do anything to jeopardise Denny's recovery. And if his and Heather's peace of mind required one of their sons to stay at the farmhouse to keep an eye on things, and if Mark was the one who had been chosen, then who was she to object?

'OK.' She inclined her head. 'Looks like we'll have to learn to get along, then.'

His strong jaw clenched and his eyes

narrowed. He leaned forward slightly on his chair. She felt her face burn under his close scrutiny and struggled to breathe.

'Don't we get on, Chrissy?'

She watched, fascinated, as he frowned. If he weren't so good-looking, he'd never get away with that. But somehow, today, the mean and moody look worked. He came across as deep and brooding, rather than bad-tempered. She bit back a smile. She shouldn't be thinking about Mark like that. Definitely not.

'Well, we're not really friends, are we?' She met his gaze and silently challenged him to disagree, her face still burning. For just a moment, she thought she spotted something in his blue eyes — he looked hurt. And she felt terrible. It wasn't that he wasn't a nice man, and he'd never been anything other than polite. She had no logical reason for feeling the way she did. Maybe it was a clash of personalities. Some people just didn't get on, did they?

But being near Mark had always

made her uneasy. Like now — though he was being perfectly proper and respectful, her skin still prickled, and she had the urge to cross her arms in a protective way across her body.

She needed to get a grip. This was all in her head; Mark had never done anything wrong. It wasn't his fault he put her on edge, after all. And she didn't want to upset him.

She was about to apologise when he shrugged his broad shoulders and his face broke into a grin. If he was handsome when he frowned, he was stunningly so when he smiled. How had she not noticed that before?

For just a moment, she forgot where she was. Or who he was. And everything about him encroaching on her territory by moving into the McGregor house to keep an eye on her. And she smiled back. He held her gaze, and she was unable to look away.

'OK, Christina Grieves, that sounds like a challenge to me. By the time my parents come home from their cruise, we'll be getting along as though we've been lifelong friends.'

'And how are we going to manage that?'

'Leave it to me,' he told her.

She shook her head, still unable to stop herself from smiling. She really couldn't see that happening. But equally, she'd talked more to him today than she had in the entire time she'd known him. Which was most of her life.

So maybe, just maybe, they could learn to get along, after all.

4

Alone With Mark

'It seems Denny McGregor doesn't trust me to do a good job on my own.' Chrissy dispensed with her usual greeting as she burst into the living room and went straight to the heart of the matter.

Her mother looked up from the magazine she was reading and frowned. 'What do you mean?'

Chrissy sighed dramatically and threw herself down on the sofa beside her mum. 'They're going away on a cruise — Heather and Denny — so Denny can recuperate properly. And they've persuaded one of the boys to move back to the farmhouse to keep an eye on things.'

Louise Grieves's eyes narrowed. 'Denny's not had a relapse, has he?'

Chrissy shook her head. 'No, thankfully. But Heather knows he won't do as the doctor said and rest if he's around the business. So she's taking him away. And they don't trust me to run the place.'

'Darling, you know they think the world of you,' Louise said. 'But looking after a business that size on your own would be a big responsibility.'

'You mean because I'm a woman and transport is a man's game?'

She could see her mother suppress a smile. 'No, I don't mean that at all. Even Denny didn't run the place on his own. He had you.'

Slightly placated by that, Chrissy sighed. 'I've managed since Denny's heart attack,' she countered.

'I know you have.'

Chrissy knew the McGregors had every right to run their business any way they saw fit, but it still hurt that they'd brought Mark in over her head. None of the McGregor boys has been interested in the transport company. Yes, Jack often advised on various matters, but even he didn't really care about the lorries and keeping the work rolling in.

But Chrissy did. She'd been passionate about the place ever since she'd hung around with Ryan when they'd been at school. When she'd been a little older, she'd even gone to work there with her father in the school holidays, where she'd helped out in the office. After she'd graduated from her business course, McGregor's Transport had been the first place she'd applied for work. And, when Denny had taken her on, she'd counted herself very lucky indeed. She'd been there ever since.

'Which son?' her mother asked now, bringing her back to the present.

Chrissy blinked. 'I'm sorry?'

Louise set her magazine down on the small table next to her and sat back, studying her daughter's features carefully. 'Which son?' Heather repeated in the face of Chrissy's silence. 'Which one have they persuaded to come home?'

'Mark,' Chrissy said with a grimace.

Her mum was thoughtful for a

moment. 'Mark's a nice lad,' she said eventually.

'I know he's nice. They're all nice. But that doesn't have anything to do with the fact they don't trust me.'

Louise patted her daughter's arm. 'You're overreacting. Of course they trust you.'

'Then why insist on Mark moving back?'

'You've been doing too much lately,' Louise told her. 'And with Denny and Heather going away, that was likely to carry on. Have you thought that maybe they've asked Mark to stay for your own good? That they're worried about asking too much of you?'

No, that hadn't occurred to her. Now she thought about it, she realised her mother had a point. But there was still one thing . . .

'Mark doesn't know anything about the business. Even the few times he's been back to visit, he's not been near the office in all the time I've worked there.'

'But he's a McGregor. And you know what Denny's like about that. If there's a McGregor on hand then he'll take the rest the doctor says he needs.'

And that was the very reason why Chrissy couldn't make a fuss. She was going to have to put up with Mark and hope that he'd keep to his word and not interfere. Not when she had the place running like clockwork.

She got to her feet. 'Shall I put the oven on and get tea started?'

'Yes, please. Juliet should be home soon. With all those extra hours she's been working, she'll be starving.'

'OK.' Chrissy mustered a smile as she got to her feet. It was obvious she wasn't about to get any sympathy from her mother. But the McGregors had been good to Louise and her daughters; and especially so since Chrissy's father had died. It was only natural that Louise would be sure their motives for bringing Mark home had been the best for all concerned.

Chrissy put her energies, instead,

into preparing an evening meal for herself, her sister, and their mother. Not that she was a particularly good cook, but she could pop a lasagne into the oven with the best of them.

Over their meal, the three chatted about their day. Chrissy was careful not to make any further complaint against the McGregors — even if she did still feel the whole matter was totally unfair.

★   ★   ★

The McGregors had always been excellent employers, as well as good friends, but Chrissy knew she couldn't bring her worries about Mark up with Denny and Heather. Not when Denny wasn't well and Heather was still so worried about him. But it didn't mean she was happy.

The day they left for their cruise, she waved them off with a smile on her face, mindful that it was her duty to make sure she didn't give them cause to worry about the place.

'Now you're sure you'll be OK with the meeting with Jackson's this afternoon?' Denny asked with a frown a mile wide.

Chrissy smiled reassuringly. Jackson's was a possible new client — a big client who could make all the difference to the financial stability of McGregor's.

'I've sat in on your sales meetings enough times,' she told him. 'And look at me — I've even worn a smart outfit. I'm taking this seriously.'

Denny nodded, acknowledging the fact that Chrissy had, indeed, made an effort to look business-like today, swapping her usual jeans for a smart skirt.

'Chrissy can cope, you know she can,' Heather told him, earning herself a grateful smile from Chrissy for the vote of confidence.

'We can phone Jack to go with you, if you need,' Denny added, obviously still not ready to let go of the reins.

'You see?' Heather said, rolling her eyes. 'This is exactly why we have to get away from here.' Chrissy and Mark both smiled.

'We'd better get going if you're going to catch this plane and join your cruise,' Mark said, ushering his parents towards his car.

Chrissy was glad he was driving them to the airport; it would mean he would be out of her hair for a couple of hours. After she'd waved them off, she went back to the office and made a concerted effort to get on with her work. As well as the normal paperwork she had to do, she needed to make sure everything was in order for the afternoon visit to Jackson's. She knew she could handle the meeting; her pitch was ready and she had all the facts and figures to hand. Being over-prepared had never caused anyone a problem as far as she was aware. With a sigh, she kept her head down and resolutely refused to think of Mark.

It was shortly after lunch when she became aware of the office door opening.

'Chrissy?'

She looked up from her computer screen to find Mark standing uncertainly in the doorway. Her heart fell. He'd promised not to interfere — and yet here he was, on the very first day.

'Yes, Mark?' she asked wearily.

He stepped inside the room and folded himself into the chair opposite Chrissy's desk. The same chair where he'd dropped his bombshell such a short time ago. He seemed reluctant to speak, though, and sat in silence for a moment before raking a hand impatiently through his mane of red hair. 'Is everything OK here?' he eventually asked.

Was he here to make idle chit-chat? Chrissy hoped she managed to hide her irritation as she nodded. 'All good, thank you.'

He took a deep breath, and she knew at once that there was more to this visit. 'I need a favour.' His frown implied he was reluctant to ask for her help.

Despite herself, she was intrigued.

40

She peered at him carefully across the desk. What could she possibly help him with? 'Do you want to tell me what you want?' she asked, careful not to commit herself one way or the other until she knew what she was dealing with.

'I wonder if I could borrow one of the vans for the afternoon — to bring my canvases and materials down from the house. My car wasn't big enough for everything.'

That seemed reasonable enough. And she was quietly pleased that he'd asked, rather than demanded. But there was only one thing . . .

'They're all out and I don't expect any of them back this side of five o'clock.'

He nodded. 'Can you pencil me in for when you have one free? I need to get my stuff as soon as I can.'

On the brink of asking why he hadn't spoken to her about this as soon as he'd discovered his parents were going away, she bit her tongue. It wasn't her business. Besides, he'd been worried about his father. And everything had been pretty rushed.

One of the bigger trucks was sitting in the yard, waiting for a service that afternoon. Mark could borrow that one — but Chrissy knew none of Denny's boys had added that class of vehicle to their licences. Her boss had grumbled about it on more than one occasion.

'I could drive you up in one of the bigger trucks,' she offered, the words out before she thought too much about it. 'As long as you don't mind if we stop off at Jackson's on the way. I don't expect the meeting to last longer than an hour.'

His eyes widened and he stared at her for a moment, seemingly shocked she'd made the offer. Which he well might be. She was a little shocked herself.

'Won't they think it odd if you turn up to meet them in a big lorry?'

She shrugged. 'We're a transport company. It comes with the territory.'

'I'd appreciate that, thank you. If

you're not too busy, of course.'

She sighed. 'I'm always busy. Come on; let's go now before I change my mind.'

The grin he flashed her way made her miss a step, and she stumbled towards him. Her face burned as she practically threw herself into his arms.

'Steady,' he told her as he reached out to stop her from falling.

'I'm not used to these heels.' She quickly stepped away, her face still on fire. And when she looked up into his face, he seemed as stunned as she felt. His smile had faded and his eyes had narrowed as he seemed to be searching her face for something. She tried to speak, but for some odd reason she couldn't.

The spell was only broken when the two collies came bounding in, looking for attention. Mark stepped away and smiled down at her, though the expression seemed forced. 'Shall we go?' he asked, sounding so cool she wondered if she'd imagined the look in his eyes only moments ago. 'The sooner we do, the sooner we can get back and both settle down to work.'

That seemed reasonable, though she still didn't trust herself to speak. She gave one short nod, grabbed the keys for the truck, and headed out of the door, without even waiting to see if he was following.

5

Road Trip

'I was planning to take the car when I got dressed this morning,' Chrissy said with a grimace as she hitched up her close-fitting skirt and prepared to climb into the cab. 'There's no way to get into one of these things elegantly.'

Mark was treated to a glimpse of her slim thigh as she pulled herself up to the driver's seat, and hated himself for the way his heart skipped a beat. Chrissy was worth so much more than that. He shook his head as he climbed in himself. As an artist, he'd painted life models on a number of occasions: women whom he'd appreciated for their undoubted beauty, but whom he had viewed in a detached manner as part of his work. Yet, one quick look at Chrissy's thigh had thrown him off balance.

Maybe it was because of what had happened in the office. He wasn't quite sure what had passed between them back there, but for the first time in all the years he'd known Chrissy, he began to suspect that maybe it wasn't dislike at the root of her discomfort around him. And he liked that thought. A lot. Too much, if he was honest.

'I have no idea where your house is,' Chrissy said, purposefully avoiding looking at him as she fiddled with the key and tried to get the truck started.

'I'll give you directions once we're out of the meeting in Aberbrig.'

She gave a short nod and he watched as her red ponytail swung about her shoulders. He'd never seen her with her hair down, but he imagined it would be spectacular. And then he told himself to stop thinking nonsense and keep this on a business footing.

Yes, he wanted Chrissy to like him — as a friend. Glancing at her exposed thigh and wondering about her hair were above and beyond the boundaries of friendship. And friendship was all he wanted for the two of them while he was staying at the McGregor farm. Anything else would make things awkward. Especially with Chrissy's reputation for giving short shrift to any man who tried any romantic nonsense around her. And no doubt there had been plenty. She was a pretty woman, so it was only natural men would notice her.

They drove to Aberbrig in near silence. He guessed she was busy mentally preparing for the meeting, and keeping the big truck on the road — that probably took a great deal of mental effort. Though she made it look easy. He silently marvelled at the way she parked the massive vehicle in a very tight space in the engineering company's car park.

'Are you coming?' she asked as she made to get out of the cab.

'Where?' He'd expected to sit outside to wait for her.

She looked at him with something

that might have been amusement. 'I can't leave a McGregor sitting in the lorry,' she told him. 'If they see you, they'll wonder what's going on.'

'But how will they know who I am?'

'Are you kidding?' She laughed. 'You have the McGregor look about you. Nobody could mistake you for anything else.'

He grinned, knowing as well as everyone else within a fifty-mile radius of Kinbrae that he looked like his dad and his brothers.

'I suppose you're right.'

★   ★   ★

Chrissy recognised her mistake as soon as the executives at Jackson's began to direct their questions towards Mark. She flirted briefly with the idea of being offended. Maybe they preferred to deal with Mark because he was a man. Although, on the other hand, she could see how someone could assume he was the one in charge — he was the one

48

who bore the company's name, after all.

Mark smiled easily in the face of all their questions. 'I'm only here as Chirssy's assistant,' he told them easily. 'I'm still learning the ropes. She's the boss.'

With that matter cleared up, the meeting went well, and Chrissy and Mark were both smiling as they set off in the lorry once again.

'You were phenomenal,' he told her quietly. 'If you don't get that contract I'll eat my hat.'

'Not good policy to count chickens,' she hurled another cliché back his way, and they both laughed.

It was good to be so relaxed in his company. For the first time ever she began to think that his promise that they would be friends one day might come true. She'd never seen him like this before; when she'd been at the yard with her dad, or when she'd hung around at the farmhouse with Ryan, Mark had either been a quiet, brooding presence, or else he'd made himself scarce.

'What way should we go?' she asked when they reached the junction at the end of the road.

'Turn right along the coast road,' he told her. 'I'll let you know when we need to turn off the road.'

She nodded and followed the directions he'd given her. 'Are we just picking up your art stuff today? Have you already brought everything else?' She kept her eyes on the road as she swung the truck back out onto the main road.

'Everything I'll need for the next few weeks,' he confirmed. 'My clothes didn't take up much room in the car.'

She nodded, still avoiding looking at him. 'You don't visit your parents often.' That had come from nowhere, and she winced as she heard his sharp intake of breath. 'I'm sorry,' she continued. 'That's none of my business.'

'No,' he agreed mildly. 'It isn't.'

She felt her face burn. Quickly, she glanced in his direction. 'I was only trying to make conversation,' she said.

'We're going to be a while driving there and back again to Kinbrae, and I don't hold with awkward silences.'

'I know.' She could hear a smile in his voice and was relieved it seemed she'd been forgiven. 'There's no reason for my lack of visits other than I travel a lot. When I'm not away, I'm at home working. And everyone's busy. I see as much of my parents as we can all manage.' She nodded. 'So, Chrissy — now I've told you one of my secrets, how about you tell me something?'

She gave a short laugh. 'That was a rubbish secret.'

She felt the air shift at her side as he shrugged a massive shoulder. 'Maybe.'

Chrissy had no secrets — nothing she wanted to hide from Mark, in any case. 'OK, Mark McGregor,' she said at last, 'what do you want to ask me about?'

'How about . . . ' He paused, and she could feel his eyes on her as she drove. ' . . . you tell me what happened between you and Sam?'

She'd been wrong. There were some

51

things she didn't want to discuss with Mark.

Had he hit a nerve? Apart from a sharp intake of breath, there was no outward sign. Unlike when she'd blushed earlier, her complexion now remained as pale as alabaster, and she didn't so much as glance across at him.

'What do you think happened with me and Sam?' she asked quietly.

He shrugged. 'I heard you threw a drink over him.'

This time she did glance across; and she must have seen his grin because she cringed, just a little. 'Ah — that.'

'Yes,' he said, 'that. Do you care to elaborate?'

He might not visit his parents often, but even he had heard of Chrissy's outrage at the behaviour of one of the drivers at the company's barbecues last summer. At the time he'd been angry she'd been subjected to Sam's drunken harassment; but his father had assured him that, as well as being publicly put in his place by Chrissy, the driver had been severely spoken to afterwards by Denny McGregor.

'He was being inappropriate.'

'In what way?'

She sighed. 'Sam got a little friendly. His advances weren't welcome.'

'Couldn't you have just told him you weren't interested?'

'The drink got the message through to him a bit quicker than words seemed to be doing.'

'Poor Sam.'

'Poor Sam, my eye,' she snapped back. 'He was trying to undermine my authority by flirting with me. I'm not above mixing with my colleagues in a social setting. I'm not, however, in the market to be chatted up.' She'd always made it clear she was at McGregor's Transport to work, not to find a boyfriend. But of course that didn't mean she hadn't met someone outside of work.

'Do you have a boyfriend?' He didn't know why he'd asked, and he immediately wished he hadn't. If she'd interpreted Sam's advances as inappropriate, there was a very good chance she might think he'd overstepped the mark. But now the question was out there, and he found he was more interested than he should have been in what her answer might be.

'Why do you ask?'

He shrugged. 'Just making conversation,' he threw her own excuse back at her. There was silence and it seemed she wasn't going to answer. 'Well?' he prompted at last. 'Do you?'

'No.'

One word, but her tone warned him not to ask anything else. So he didn't. Besides, they were at the place where the coast road had veered far from the sea, and they'd need to turn toward his house soon. It was time for him to start giving directions.

'We need to turn left in about a hundred yards,' he said, trying to sound as though he wasn't delighted she wasn't seeing anyone. Which he shouldn't be — not when he knew Chrissy was off-limits for so many reasons. No matter how green her eyes, or how lovely her face. And she was definitely not interested in him — he could see that beyond doubt now. He must have imagined that expression in her eyes earlier.

Wordlessly, she turned the truck up the sharp incline of a narrow, tree-lined lane that would lead them up to the cliffs. A few miles along, they emerged from the greenery and he couldn't suppress a smile when she sighed as the view hit her square between the eyes.

'It's spectacular,' she said almost to herself as his house came into view. Overlooking the sea, it was a phenomenon of modern architecture, made of stone and glass that somehow blended in with the surroundings.

He was pleased she liked it. He hardly ever had anyone back to the house; and even on the few occasions someone did make it past his inherent need to be alone, he couldn't care less what they thought of his place.

But, with Chrissy, it mattered a great deal.

6

Growing Closer

Chrissy followed Mark as he led the way to the side of the building and unlocked the door, before quickly making his way to a control panel and punching in the code to disable the alarm.

'The insurance company insisted,' he said, giving a little shrug, almost as though he was embarrassed by the fuss. 'They wouldn't insure my paintings without it.'

'But you're miles away from anywhere. Who'd hear an alarm all the way out here?'

'Nobody, apart from potential burglars. But it's linked to a security company; they ring the house if it goes off, and if I don't give them a password they contact the police.'

She gave a short nod. She'd heard about his paintings, of course, and all the talk had been favourable. She knew he made a good living, so it was sensible that he took measures to protect his work.

They went into Mark's studio — a large, airy room with a wall of glass overlooking the sea, letting in an abundance of natural light. She looked around at his paintings, some half-done, some finished. And she felt a shiver run down her back. Chrissy had always been a practical sort of person; a businesswoman first and foremost, who loved nothing more than dealing with facts and figures. Art had never touched her before. But looking at Mark's work was a surreal experience; she felt connected to him in a way she'd never expected.

'They're all seascapes,' she said as she wandered from one to the other.

'That's the theme for this next exhibition,' he told her.

Something wasn't right. She felt her

brow crease as she looked across at him. 'How can you paint the sea at the farm?' She waved towards the window and the sea beyond it. 'Don't you need this to be inspired?'

He grinned and she felt another shiver down her spine. 'As long as I'm inspired in here,' he said, raising his hand to his chest, 'I can paint anywhere.'

She could see exactly what he meant as she glanced at his work again. His paintings had heart. That was why they had touched her so deeply. 'So you'll sell all of these?' she asked.

'That's the plan. If the exhibition goes well.'

She shook her head. 'I don't know how you can bear to part with them.'

'Is that a compliment?' he asked, his eyes on her face.

'Of course it's a compliment. These are wonderful.'

He grinned. 'Thank you.'

Embarrassed, she looked away. 'We should get going,' she told him. 'What do you need to bring? I'll give you a hand.'

He directed her towards some of the smaller bags containing brushes and paints, while he moved the larger canvases. Very soon they had everything he needed loaded onto the truck.

'Are you sure the place will be OK?' she asked. 'If anyone knows it's empty, might they try to break in?'

'The place is secure,' he said as he set the alarm.

'It would be a disaster if anyone stole any of the paintings you've already finished.'

'It would,' he agreed. 'But they won't be here unattended for long. I'll need to send them to the gallery soon.'

And, because he wasn't worried, she decided there was no need for her to be, either.

It didn't take long for Chrissy to make sure everything was safely strapped down before they set off. But they'd barely made it to the end of the driveway before the vehicle spluttered to a halt. 'Oh, no.'

Chrissy couldn't believe this. She jumped from the cab and had a look at the engine.

'What is it?' Mark asked, coming out to stand beside her.

She glanced over her shoulder to find him close — too close. And his brow furrowed as he, too, peered at the engine.

'It's my fault.' Chrissy had a sinking feeling in the pit of her stomach, but she knew she had to make the confession. 'I'm so sorry. This truck's been giving us bother. The mechanic was due to give it a service later this afternoon; that's why it was still sitting in the yard. I thought it would be OK for one journey, but I guess my optimism's caught up with me.'

His eyes darkened and seemed to see into her soul, and she braced herself for Mark's anger. She'd be furious in his place, especially as she knew he had work to do. But the expected response never quite materialised. He sighed quietly and ran a hand through his hair.

Then his lips twitched into something that looked very much like it might be a smile.

'These things happen,' he said quite reasonably. 'And I suppose I should take at least half the blame. If I hadn't wanted to fetch my things at such short notice, you wouldn't have felt obliged to bring this lorry out.'

That surprised her. Pleasantly so. Mark might not have the jokey manner of his brothers, or the same way of making her feel like one of the lads, but his sharing the blame for something that had been her mistake instantly elevated him in her eyes. She felt her own lips curve in response as the sea breeze cooled her cheeks.

'I think, Mark McGregor, that you're a bit of a gentleman on the quiet.' She nearly laughed out loud at his surprised expression, but instead managed to control herself long enough to dig her mobile from her jacket pocket. 'And, before you ask, yes,' she told him, 'that was another compliment. Most of the guys would never let me live this down.'

She'd expected him to laugh, but he didn't. His expression was deadly serious as his brilliant blue eyes clashed with her green ones. And she forgot to breathe for a minute.

They were on the cliff top, overlooking the most spectacular scenery imaginable, with the sea breeze gently kissing their faces. And Chrissy was oblivious to everything apart from the man who was standing only feet away from her.

It seemed Mark was equally enthralled. Without taking his eyes from hers, he took a step towards her. And, before she knew it, she was in his arms.

If anyone had suggested five minutes ago that she would be kissing Mark McGregor as though her life depended on it, she would have laughed in their face.

But now it was actually happening, nothing in the world made more sense.

Mark reluctantly lifted his lips from Chrissy's and took a dazed step back. 'I'm sorry,' he said. 'That shouldn't have happened.'

He didn't know how it had happened. One minute they'd been talking about the lorry and she'd been about to phone the mechanic, and then . . .

But she *had* kissed him back. She looked up at him now, seemingly speechless, which had to be a first for Chrissy.

He gave silent thanks that there were no handy beverages around. If there were, he had no doubt he'd now be dripping wet, like the unfortunate Sam. And rightly so. Because, even if she had kissed him back, it was still his fault — he'd kissed her first.

'I think,' she said breathlessly, 'if we're going to share the blame for the lorry breaking down, we should share the blame for this, too.' She turned away so he could no longer see the soft blush that warmed her cheeks.

'I should call the breakdown service,' he said, trying to act normally so he didn't embarrass her further. 'Ask them to come and take a look at the truck.

Do you have the number?'

She nodded and waved the phone that was still in her hand; but rather than hand it over, she made the call herself. She quickly explained what the matter was and where they were, then she hung up. When she turned back towards Mark, her green eyes were bright and there was still a soft blush on her cheeks, but thankfully she didn't look angry. He hadn't offended her.

'The mechanic will be here as soon as he can.' She grimaced. 'But he said it would be at least a couple of hours because he's already on an urgent job.'

Mark nodded. He knew she was busy and couldn't afford to be away from the office for that length of time, but there was very little that could be done about it now.

'Shall we go back to the house and sit it out in comfort?' And again he liked the idea of entertaining Chrissy in his home. In fact, he liked it even more now he knew how good she'd felt in his arms; how sweet her kiss had tasted.

She nodded, and it only took them a minute to reach his house.

'Would you like something to drink?' he asked, vaguely aware he might be asking for trouble. She might have been insistent earlier on sharing the blame for their kiss, but she might change her mind and hurl the drink after all. And, in his own opinion, he still deserved to be rebuked for his part in it. Despite the fact he'd kiss her again in a heartbeat, Chrissy deserved better. She deserved to be romanced and cherished. Even though she presented a tough exterior, deep down he'd always known that about her. Mark was no romantic where women were concerned; he reserved his sensitive side for his art.

'Thank you. I'd love some water, please.'

He went to the fridge and took out a couple of bottles of mineral water, then found glasses for them both. 'If the mechanic's going to be a couple of hours, it might be best if we had something to eat, too. It'll be late by the time we get back.' He tried to make the suggestion sound casual — as though everything was normal, and his world hadn't changed forever a few moments ago with a kiss.

Because it had. And he didn't know how he was going to be able to spend so much time with Chrissy at the farmhouse when all they were supposed to be was friends. And, as far as she was concerned, they weren't even that.

As he watched her, a slow smile curved her full lips. 'Yes, thank you, Mark. That's a good idea.'

And he knew he was in trouble when even the sound of his name on her lips had his heart beating a little faster.

★ ★ ★

Voices greeted Chrissy as she let herself into the house that night. At first she thought it must be her mother and sister chatting in the kitchen. But, after taking off her coat and making her way through the living room, she realised

66

the person her mother was talking to wasn't Juliet but their neighbour, Joyce Imrie.

Despite being exhausted after the events of the day, she smiled. She liked Joyce and was keen to catch up. She was about to join the two women when her mother's concerned voice reached her.

'I worry that it's because of what happened with me that Chrissy's the way she is.'

'What do you mean?' Joyce asked. 'What way is Chrissy?'

'Well, you know,' her mother said, 'the way she's always been around men. She never wants to get involved. Doesn't want to get married — not ever, she says. I worry that's because when her dad died she was at an impressionable age. And then, of course, there's been my disaster of a dating history since we lost Anthony. That's bound to have made an impression.'

'Didn't she go out with that farm boy a while back?'

'You mean Angus?'

'That's the one.'

Her mother's sigh reached her. 'It wasn't anything romantic. Though I suspect he would have liked it to be. And he was lovely. If she couldn't form a relationship with him, there has to be something to worry about.'

She heard Joyce tut loudly. 'There's nothing wrong with Chrissy. She just won't settle for a man who's not good enough for her — she'll be waiting for someone special. And there's nothing the matter with that.'

She heard her mother sigh loudly again. 'I suppose you're right.'

Chrissy frowned. She knew she couldn't hang around in the living room listening at the door. What she'd heard so far she could put down to an accident; but if she lingered any longer, she would be eavesdropping on purpose. And she'd never been one to sneak around.

Though she was slightly stunned by her mother's perceptive summary. Louise had never once mentioned to her daughter that she was worried Chrissy didn't date. It was true Kinbrae wasn't known for its hot men, but Chrissy had decided a long time ago to keep away from romance. During the months and years she'd watched her mother struggle as a widowed parent to two young girls, that seed had been firmly planted.

When she'd grown a little older, she'd realised her mother was still grieving, even after so many years. And every failed relationship had been the result of her search to find someone to replace the husband who'd died.

It was as a teenager that Chrissy had resolved never to allow any man that kind of power over her. Yes, her parents had been happy and in love once; but when Louise had been left with two young daughters, life had been harsh.

Though, in Mark's arms, she'd had a taste of what it might be like to allow herself to be swept away. She sighed. Now was not the time to think of him — or of how his kiss had made her toes tingle. Or how something in the back of her mind nagged that Mark would be the kind of man a girl could rely on.

Forcing a bright smile so neither her mother nor Joyce would suspect she'd overheard the conversation, she crashed loudly into the kitchen. 'Hello,' she told them brightly. 'I had a terrible time at work today. I got held up when one of the lorries broke down. I think I'm going to have to put in a couple of hours over the weekend.'

Her mother looked dismayed. 'You work too hard,' she said.

Chrissy shrugged. 'It keeps me out of mischief.'

'That's true enough — you'd have no time to get up to no good with the hours you work.' Joyce smiled and got to her feet. 'I'd best get going. Alice has invited me over for dinner tonight and I mustn't be late.'

Alice, Joyce's twin sister, had recently married her childhood sweetheart. The couple had met after many years apart, when Alice had moved back to stay with Joyce after decades away from Kinbrae.

'Oh, how lovely,' Louise said with a smile. 'Tell Alice and Trevor we were asking after them.'

'Thank you, I will,' Joyce promised as she put on her coat and picked up her handbag.

In a way, Chrissy felt sorry for Joyce: to be alone again when her sister had retired and moved to Kinbrae so that she could keep her company must hurt. But on the other hand, Alice was so visibly happy that it would be nearly impossible for anyone to be displeased by the situation.

7

Lunch Al Fresco

Mark breathed the cool morning air deeply into his lungs as he arrived back in the yard, the two dogs running ahead. He had a sudden urge to paint the hills that surrounded his parents' home, though he knew he'd have to get his seascapes finished first if he was to meet the deadline for his exhibition.

This wasn't a bad place, he realised. He'd been happy as a child. And it was possible to attain the solitude his artist's soul craved even here. His walk across the field with the two collies, Bob and Florence, had reminded him of that.

Then he remembered why he'd left — it might be peaceful this Saturday morning, but on a work day the place was noisy and busy. And he'd needed peace inside his own head to think about his work. He needed space to create.

He'd made a home for himself somewhere else now: a place where he could wallow in that necessary solitude and still take off with a moment's notice, without having to explain himself to anyone. But on mornings like this, when the farmyard was empty of the drivers who would normally be calling out to each other, and with the lorries idle instead of noisily driving to and fro, he could see that he had everything he needed here.

'Let's go and see to your breakfast,' he told the two dogs as they walked to the house.

The dew was still damp on his boots, and he was preparing to take them off on the doorstep, when he heard a car in the distance. His senses were immediately on alert, as the vehicle seemed to be approaching. There were no deliveries scheduled for today; he'd expected to be alone. And there was only one person he could think of who might drive up here at this time on a weekend morning.

A glance over his shoulder confirmed what his subconscious had suggested: it was Chrissy's car, now making its way down the track towards the farmhouse.

He hadn't expected to see her today. Chrissy was entitled to time off just like everyone else, especially when she worked so hard during the week. He smiled as she brought her car to a stop. He couldn't help it, even though he knew their friendship was still on shaky ground.

He forgot everything about taking his boots off and walked back out into the farmyard. It was odd — watching her drive towards the house had felt almost as though a part of him he hadn't known was missing had returned. Which was ridiculous. Maybe the early morning walk had gone to his head.

She opened the car door, and both dogs left his side and bounded up to her, barking their greetings as Chrissy got out. She laughed as she petted them, and Mark thought he'd never seen her look so lovely.

But then she glanced up and caught him staring. Immediately her laughter faded and her expression became guarded. 'Hi,' she said, almost shyly.

If he didn't know Chrissy better, he'd have guessed she'd been avoiding him over the past few days — since she'd taken him to fetch his things and he'd kissed her senseless in an unforgivably weak moment. But he knew hiding from her problems wasn't Chrissy's style, so that couldn't be the case.

She'd been busy — and he'd felt a pang of guilt as he'd realised he'd added to her workload by asking for help to fetch his things. In fact, he wouldn't be at all surprised if that was why she felt the need to work today — to make up for lost time.

'Hi,' he replied. 'Wasn't expecting to see you today.'

'No.' She took more interest than was strictly necessary as she continued to pat the dogs' heads. 'I just have a few things to finish up in the office.'

He'd known she wasn't there to see him — every rational bone in his body had told him that. But he was still a little disappointed, he realised, at the confirmation that she really was there to work.

He gave a short nod. 'Well, let me get these two out of your way. I'll do the rounds feeding the animals, then be in the barn if you need me.'

But he didn't move. And neither did she. In reality, they probably stood there for no more than a minute, but it seemed like a lifetime. Mark gazed into her face and, even though he knew he should turn and walk away, he seemed incapable of going anywhere. In that instant he wanted to do nothing more than gather her up in his arms again. If he were honest, he'd thought a lot about the kiss they'd shared at his place, and he was very interested in finding out if she would be agreeable to a repeat experience.

He was on the brink of taking a step towards her when he felt something against his hand. The spell broken, he glanced down to find Florence nuzzling against him.

'Looks like someone wants her breakfast,' Chrissy said. He looked back up to find her smiling. Then she turned and walked into the house, and towards her office, without a backward glance.

Chrissy was sure she shouldn't look back. That would only encourage him, and that would be wrong when encouraging him was the last thing she wanted to do. And, once she was in the office, she made a huge effort to put him out of her mind. The paperwork was her priority and she had to get it done, or else forcing herself to come into the office this early on a Saturday morning would have been for nothing.

It wasn't as though she hadn't had lots of practice being single-minded — her job had always been her priority. And work was a much more reliable obsession than a man.

She closed her eyes, took a deep breath, and focused. Then she worked like a demon for the rest of the morning.

When there was a knock at the office door she nearly jumped out of her skin. 'Yes?' she called out — and wasn't at all surprised to see Mark pop his head around the door. Who else would it be when the two of them were here alone?

'I've made lunch,' he said, looking quite pleased with himself. 'I was planning to take it down by the river — kill two birds by getting some fresh air at the same time.' He glanced towards the window. 'Have to make the most of this weather.'

She frowned. 'Why are you telling me this?'

'There's enough for two. I wondered if you'd like to join me?'

It was on the tip of her tongue to refuse; she had a ton of work to do. Besides, she didn't need to spend any more time alone with him. If her recent behaviour was anything to go by, she seemed incapable of self-control around him, and she might end up kissing him again. Giving him the wrong idea. Again.

But her stomach chose that moment to issue a loud grumbling complaint about how long it had been since her hurriedly snatched breakfast.

He grinned. 'Will I take that as a yes?'

She smiled back. She couldn't help it. 'Yes, please.'

She'd just have to make an effort to control the urge to kiss him for half an hour while they ate. Then she'd be straight back in here, out of harm's way.

★   ★   ★

When they arrived at the river, Mark considered what a pleasant surprise it had been when Chrissy had agreed to join him. He'd hoped she would, of course; and he wouldn't have made the extra food if he hadn't wanted her to. But when he'd first extended the invitation, she'd looked almost fierce. Then when she'd smiled, he'd almost forgotten to breathe.

'Are you having to work today because you lost time when you helped me fetch my gear?' he asked as he arranged a rug on the grass under a large oak tree on the riverbank.

She was always so busy. It stood to reason that hours away from work would have to be made up. And he felt guilty that she was having to put in these hours of unpaid overtime because of him.

'Partly,' she admitted, and his guilt intensified a hundred percent. 'But I lost a few hours at the meeting and doing some extra deliveries, too.'

There was an easy silence as they ate.

'Will you be here all day?' Mark asked as he began to tidy the remains of their picnic into the wicker basket he'd found at the back of the pantry. This basket had served the McGregors well over the years, and it brought back many happy memories of family picnics in this very spot. After today, he was sure it would bring back memories of a different kind for him.

She didn't reply straight away, and after a moment he glanced up to find she was watching him carefully. 'Does it bother you that I'm here today?' she asked him.

He sighed. Even now, after sharing this relaxed lunch, she was so prickly; so quick to take his words the wrong way. He knew for a fact she'd never been like that with Jack or Ryan. And he regretted the quiet demeanour that made him awkward around women. Or, rather, around this woman in particular — because he'd never before wished to impress anyone the way he wanted to impress Chrissy right now.

'I like you being here,' he told her quietly. 'Maybe I like having you around a bit too much.'

He watched as her eyes widened and a soft blush made her cheeks glow. 'Is this part of your offensive in operation let's-be-friends?'

He laughed. 'You've seen through me.'

Slowly, uncertainly at first, she joined in his laughter, and Mark knew a rare minute of perfect contentment. 'I only wondered,' he said, desperate to prolong the moment, 'if you'd be around for dinner?'

She shook her head. 'I don't think so. I've got another couple of hours to do, then I'd better be going.'

'No problem.'

Her eyes narrowed as she looked at him. 'Were you asking me on a date, Mark McGregor?'

'Just dinner — shared with a friend,' he supplied smoothly, guessing she wouldn't appreciate it if he told her that a date had been exactly what he'd had in mind.

'Good, because I've no interest in dating. And I don't expect you to cook me dinner. Lunch was more than I was expecting.'

'It's no trouble. I enjoy preparing food and I don't often get the chance to cook for anyone else. I only thought if you were free, it would be nice to have the company.'

She smiled, a lid midway to the tub of pasta salad she was tidying away. His heart gave the tiny flutter that was becoming a little too familiar around Chirssy Grieves. 'If your dinners are as tasty as lunch,' she said, 'then I'd be an idiot to turn your offer down.'

Ah, so that was the key — the way to her heart was through her stomach. And, thanks to his mother insisting that all her boys were handy around the house, and his stint as a teenager working at McGregor's Café, he could more than hold his own in the kitchen. Maybe he'd found the perfect way to impress her after all.

'So . . . tonight?' He held his breath as he waited for her response.

There was a smile about her lips as she nodded. 'OK, why not?'

'Good. Dinner for two it is, then.'

★ ★ ★

Mark was preoccupied for the rest of the day. Chrissy had wondered if his friendly gestures had been part of a plan; a way to win her friendship so he could prove a point. But wanting to win her approval and good opinion had nothing to do with the promise he'd made her the day his parents had asked him to move in here. And it had everything to do with the way he felt about Chrissy. If he were honest with himself — and he was finally in a place where he could be — he'd always liked her. So it was no wonder that her aloof behaviour around him had always hurt. Now that he could recognise that truth and admit his feelings, he could also admit that getting to know her better, and persuading her to trust him, was starting to mean everything to him.

He gave up all pretence of work and put his paintbrush aside as he heaved a sigh into the too-quiet barn. When his brothers had been courting, he'd watched from a distance, bemused. He hadn't been able to understand at all why they had allowed their worlds to be turned upside down — even though Paula and Vicky were both lovely. But now he could understand exactly what the fuss was about. Because a woman like Chrissy was worth making an effort for.

His mother had left plenty of food: the cupboards were full and there were meals already prepared in the freezer. But he wanted to make Chirssy something special. He knew that what she'd agreed to wasn't a date as such, but there was zero chance he'd be able to concentrate on his painting this afternoon. So it made sense that he should go shopping for the ingredients for a meal.

Without giving himself a chance to think, he found himself outside the office, and rapping neatly at the door before popping his head round. Chrissy looked up, and he thought he saw something flash in her green eyes. But before he could be sure, it was gone and she was glaring with cool detachment.

'Yes?'

'Just heading out for while. I'll be back in time to prepare dinner.'

She gave a short nod as though she really couldn't care either way. And he smiled, because he had seen another side to her at his home when she'd helped him move his art supplies, and at lunch earlier that day. He was sure that things between them were moving in the right direction — even if she wasn't quite admitting it out loud yet.

And there it was: A hint of a smile in return that made her full lips curve ever so slightly, and her eyes light up. 'See you later,' she said softly.

He walked back past the barn towards his car, and was startled when someone emerged from inside the building. 'Sam,' he said as he recognised the driver. 'I didn't expect to see you there. I didn't think any of you drivers were in today.'

'Yeah. Just going,' Sam said, looking shifty.

'What were you doing in the barn?' Mark asked when Sam made to walk away.

The other man looked a little sheepish. 'Thought I'd have a look at your paintings,' he said. 'I heard the others talking — they said each one was worth thousands.'

Mark took a deep breath. He didn't like the way this man was speaking. Whatever his paintings were worth, it was none of Sam's business.

'They're only worth what someone is willing to pay for them,' he told Sam.

Sam gave a short nod.

'Just one thing,' he added as Sam went to walk off again.

'What?'

'I prefer to keep the work under wraps until the official opening of the exhibition. So I'd appreciate if you didn't go into the barn again until I move my things out.' What he'd told Sam was true, with the noticeable exception to this rule of Chrissy. He hadn't minded her seeing his half finished work.

Sam didn't look impressed. His lip curled, almost in a snarl. But even though Mark had tried to be nice about it, there was no getting away from the fact that Sam had no business wandering around the place on a Saturday, or being in any of the outbuildings.

'Whatever you say,' Sam said gruffly before he turned and strutted off towards the lane.

Mark took the time to lock the barn before he left. Even though Sam had gone, the incident had concerned him. And he was still frowning as he drove from the farmyard. He didn't like to leave Chrissy on her own — not now he knew Sam had been wandering around the place. Even though he was certain the other man had gone for now, he decided he'd best be quick about this shopping trip.

He realised, though, that the small village of Kinbrae wasn't likely to have what he was looking for. So when he got to the end of the lane, he turned towards the larger town of Aberbrig. Once there, he quickly picked up the ingredients to make his signature seafood lasagne — something he hoped

Chrissy would like.

As soon as he drove back into the farmyard he could sense there was something wrong. And that suspicion was confirmed when he got out of the car and the dogs didn't come up to greet him.

'Chrissy.' Her name tore from his lips as he ran towards the house. He knew he shouldn't have left her alone.

8

A Medical Emergency

There was no sign of her in the house. Papers littered her desk, but that was nothing unusual, as she often left her work out to finish the next time she was in. Mark knew bitter disappointment as he realised she must have gone home.

After putting his shopping away, he put on the kettle, then opened the kitchen window to let in some air. It was then that he heard the voices. There were people in the field next to the farmhouse. His parents had been renting the land out for years, to a neighbouring farmer. It had seemed pointless to keep it when the lorries had, at that time, been doing pretty well for themselves. At first Mark thought the farmer and his workers must be there fixing a fence or something. But as he listened, he realised one of the voices sounded remarkably like Chrissy's. And she also sounded upset.

Following the noise, he headed outside towards the gate that still remained from the farmyard to the field beyond. He had to push his way through overgrowth — this access hadn't been used properly in years, as Angus always reached the field from his own land.

For a moment, Mark stood immobile at the sight that greeted him: there was a tractor on its side and Chirssy was on her knees next to it, the two dogs by her side. And, between her and the tractor, Angus the farmer was lying on the ground.

Galvanised into action, Mark shot across to where they were. 'What happened?' Daft question. He could see what had happened.

'It was getting warm, so I went to open the office window to let in some air and I heard Angus calling,' Chrissy told him. 'He'd been here a while.'

'Forgot to bring my mobile,' Angus

said as he grimaced at the tractor. 'I hit an uneven patch of ground and the tractor flipped over.'

'Where are you hurt?'

'Everywhere.' Angus gave a groan. 'I can't get up.'

Mark could see from the angle of Angus's leg that it was probably broken, but he knew there might well be further damage to his back. 'Well, don't try to move.'

'The ambulance should be here soon,' Chrissy told him, her face pale and her voice shaky.

When the siren sounded a few minutes later, Mark went back to the farmyard to direct the paramedics to the patient.

Soon, Angus was being carefully moved onto a stretcher, and then out to where the ambulance waited for him in front of the McGregor farmhouse, which was the closest point it could reach without going off road. Chrissy followed, still pale and unusually subdued — shock, Mark imagined.

'I'm going with him,' she said, walking purposefully towards the ambulance. 'We can't let him go alone. We don't know how badly he's hurt.'

'Of course,' he said, cross with himself for not thinking of it. But he did think about Chrissy arriving at the hospital and sitting on her own — maybe for quite a while — as she waited for news. And then she'd have to make her own way home somehow, with her car still here at the farmhouse.

He waited until the ambulance had driven out of sight before breaking into action. Not knowing how long they would be at the hospital, he hurriedly fed the animals, then got into his car and headed towards Aberbrig.

* * *

The first person Mark saw when he went through the hospital doors was his younger brother, who worked there as an A&E nurse. 'Have you seen Chrissy?' he asked as Ryan headed over to him.

Ryan nodded towards the waiting area. 'She's over there, waiting for news about Angus.'

Mark glanced over, and his heart lurched as he spotted a familiar red ponytail. 'She seems pretty upset,' he said, taking in how pale Chrissy still was. 'But I suppose finding someone thrown from a tractor would be a shock for anyone.'

'Especially when it's an ex-boyfriend,' Ryan said.

Mark felt his jaw clench. 'They used to go out?' He wondered why he hadn't known about this. But then he wasn't home much and didn't make a habit of listening to gossip.

Ryan nodded. 'It ended suddenly last year. I don't know what happened.'

Mark didn't know why that bothered him so much. Or maybe he did — because that seemed to indicate that, far from not wanting a relationship, Chrissy just didn't want a relationship with him.

But it was selfish to think like that now. A man had been hurt, possibly quite badly. Once he knew Angus was going to be OK, there would be plenty of time to think about himself and Chrissy, and to wonder at why she seemed intent on keeping him at a distance.

'I don't suppose there's any news yet?' he asked his brother.

Ryan shook his head. 'Not yet. The doctor's with him now. Hopefully we'll know something before long.'

'It didn't look good,' Mark said, not daring to let his mind dwell too long on the possibilities of the harm that could befall a farmer who tangled with a tractor.

'No,' Ryan agreed. 'But he's young and strong, and at least he was thrown clear. If anyone can pull through this it will be him.'

Mark gave a short nod and went over to join Chrissy. She looked up at him with expectant green eyes as he approached. 'I saw you talking to Ryan.' The question, while unspoken, was clearly etched in the furrows on her forehead.

He wished he had news that would make her frown fade. He didn't like to see her worried. 'No news yet. They hope it won't be too much longer before they know something.' He glanced around as a thought occurred. 'Should we call his family?' Angus had a widowed mother who lived with him, and a younger sister. It was only right that they be told of his condition.

'His mum's away visiting her friend for a few days,' Chrissy said. 'But Alexandra's on her way. She works in Aberbrig, so she should be here before too long.'

It was only moments later that Alexandra joined them in the waiting area. As small as her brother was big, she had the same brown eyes and dark, unruly hair, though hers was considerably longer. 'How is he?' she demanded at once. 'Can I see him?'

'The doctor's with him,' Mark told her. 'They'll let us know when there's news.'

'What happened?' She was obviously striving to make sense of the situation as she looked from Mark to Chrissy and back again.

'Come and sit down,' Chrissy told her gently, 'and I'll explain what we know.'

'And I'll go and fetch us some tea,' Mark suggested. To be honest, he was glad to have a practical task to complete. Something positive to do. He was no good with words, or with sitting still and offering silent sympathy. He was no good, either, at showing empathy, unless it was with a paint-brush on canvas. He was much better doing something while they waited — even if it was only acting as tea boy. It was at times like this when he envied his brother's calling to be a nurse. Ryan was never at a loss in an emergency; he was equipped and trained to help and to make a difference.

'Hi, Mark. What are you doing here?' He looked around to find Faye, one of the nurses his brother shared a house with. Though of course Ryan wouldn't be living in that place much longer: he and Vicky were making plans to find a place of their own once they were married.

'Faye.' He nodded a greeting as they walked together towards the tea machine. 'A neighbour was involved in an accident.'

'And you brought him in?'

'Nothing so heroic. I followed the ambulance. My . . . ' He paused. What exactly was Chrissy to him? He knew she wanted to keep him at a distance — and yet she was so much more than an employee of McGregor Transport. 'My friend,' he decided defiantly, 'came in with him, and she'll need a lift back.'

Faye nodded. 'Was that Chrissy I saw in the waiting area? Is that who you're talking about? Is she your friend?'

He'd forgotten that they knew each other; they'd both been at Jack and Paula's wedding for a start. And no doubt they'd bumped into each other countless other times he wasn't aware of, too.

'Yes, it's Chrissy,' he said, his lips involuntarily curving into a hint of a smile as he spoke her name.

He knew he'd given too much away when Faye gave him a knowing look, seeming to put her own interpretation onto his expression. He knew he should deny the silent allegation; Chrissy wouldn't thank him for giving out the wrong impression. But what could he say? If he protested that they were only friends, Faye would read so much more into it.

'Can I get you some tea?' he asked, deciding that changing the subject was the safest option.

'No, I'm all right, thank you.' She glanced at her watch. 'I was on my way back from my break, and if I don't hurry I'll be late. I hope there's good news about your neighbour.'

'Thanks.'

'And say hi to your *friend* for me.' She grinned as she turned and walked briskly back to work.

★ ★ ★

'Cuts, bruises, and a broken leg.' Chrissy's voice was barely more than a whisper.

Mark took his eyes off the road for a second and glanced across at her. She was still pale, her green eyes anxious.

'If he hadn't been thrown from the tractor, it could have been worse,' he told her. 'He was lucky the cab only clipped him on the way down.'

'Yes, we need to be grateful.'

It had been a horrible day for all of them — worse for Angus, of course. But Chrissy's experience must have been very stressful, too: finding an ex-boyfriend, someone she'd loved, injured beside a huge piece of overturned farm machinery.

'Do you want to stop for something to eat?' he asked, knowing McGregor's Café would have closed by now. It would make sense to stop in one of the restaurants in Aberbrig if they were going have a meal.

She sighed. 'I couldn't face food just now.'

He glanced over at her again. She looked exhausted. 'OK. I'll take you straight home and fetch you in the morning so you can pick up your car.'

'Are you sure? I don't want to put you out. You've already lost half a day's work today.'

'Not a problem,' he assured her with far more confidence than he felt. He really needed to concentrate and get the collection finished.

'We're going to need to do something about Angus's farm,' she said thoughtfully. 'Help in some way. It will take him a while to recover.'

He negotiated a sharp bend and they started to climb the first hill out of town and towards Kinbrae. 'He has workers on the farm, doesn't he?'

'Yes, two full-time farmhands,' Chrissy replied. 'But he did a lot of the work himself. There's no way Joe and Campbell will cope on their own.' He nodded. 'Lexi will help, of course,' she continued. 'But she does have a job of her own, so she won't be available for the entire time Angus will need help.'

'I'll speak to Joe and Campbell,' he

said. 'Once we get a better idea of what they need, we'll know what we can do to help.' Even though he knew it would be difficult to take time away from his own work, there was no way he could leave the farm next door in the lurch. Helping out in times of need was what neighbours did.

However much he tried to concentrate on the problem, though, his mind kept wandering back to the fact that Chrissy had once been in a relationship with Angus. Mark had never been a jealous or a possessive man. In fact, the women he'd dated had — without exception — ended the relationships because he was too reluctant to make a commitment. He was too laid-back, they'd all said. He never made them feel as though they were his girlfriends. So this brooding feeling over Chrissy and Angus made no sense.

At last, they were driving into Kinbrae. He knew he had no business saying anything, but the urge to talk about it was stronger than he was.

'Ryan told me . . . ' he began as he pulled the car to the side of the road outside her house.

Her eyes were wide as she looked across at him and her nose wrinkled. 'Told you what?'

He sighed. He knew they really shouldn't be having this conversation. It was none of his business. He might be falling for her, but she'd hadn't encouraged him at all. Well, there had been that kiss — his mind wandered for a moment as he appreciated the memory. But apart from that . . .

'About you and Angus.'

When she blushed, he knew that it was true. 'That wasn't anything much. We went out for a while, but it was pretty obvious we were on a different page.'

'In what way?'

'He was looking for a farmer's wife. And, like I said to you, I'm not looking for anything like that.' She smiled, and for a moment Mark felt as though he was falling though space.

'He's still not married, though.'

'No, he's not.' She shrugged. 'I guess he's still looking.'

'Do you think he's hoping you'll change your mind?'

Her soft sigh filled the space inside the car. 'I've never given him any reason to think I might.' Large eyes looked directly at him for a moment in the evening light. Then she turned her head and snapped off her seatbelt. 'Thanks for the lift.' She glanced over her shoulder and gave him a tight little smile, and a cool rush of night air hit his face as she left the car. He stopped for a moment and watched as she walked down the path. She turned just as she reached the door and gave a little wave.

He lifted his own hand in acknowledgement. And, despite her assurance, he couldn't help wondering if maybe Angus still harboured feelings towards Chrissy. And if maybe she wasn't quite over him.

He shook his head and put his car into gear. 'None of your business,' he told himself out loud as he drove off.

9

Remaining Aloof

Juliet was alone and sitting in the living room, watching a film. 'Mum's gone out with the girls.' She barely looked up from the screen.

Chrissy didn't like the sound of that. The last time their mother had gone out with the girls, she'd met one of her mismatched suitors. But Juliet seemed happy enough with the situation, so Chrissy decided there was no point in upsetting her sister.

'What are you doing home on a Saturday night?' Chirssy asked, dropping onto the sofa.

'Don't make me sound like such a loser,' her sister retorted. 'You're home, too.'

Chrissy picked up a cushion and threw it. Her sister caught it neatly and grinned.

'Felt like a quiet night,' Juliet admitted. 'That party lot are getting a bit rowdy for me. Must be maturing.'

'This is what happens when people hit their twenties.' Chrissy stared mindlessly at the television for a few moments. It had been a hard day: she hadn't managed half the work she'd hoped to get through, and was emotionally and physically drained.

'Angus had an accident,' she shared at last.

Her sister sat up. 'Is he OK?'

'Not really, but he will be.'

'What happened?'

'He tangled with his tractor and lost. He's in hospital.'

Chrissy had always known that her sister was fond of Angus, but her reaction now surprised her: the colour drained from the younger woman's face. 'Is anyone with him?' Juliet asked.

'Lexi was there when Mark and I left. He's hoping he'll be sent home once they've seen to his injuries.'

That news seemed to calm Juliet

down a little and she sat back, seemingly engrossed in the film. But Chrissy could see her sister's hands wringing together on her lap. 'Is there something you're not telling me?' she asked at last.

Juliet shook her head. 'Not a thing. Look, I'm tired. I think I'll turn in, too.'

'But it's only ten o'clock.'

'I've had a busy day.'

And so Chrissy was alone. She should probably retire for the evening, too. She was going to have to put a couple of hours in at the office again in the morning. And she wanted to head up to the farm early — on foot, so that Mark didn't have to come and fetch her.

She started to switch off lamps and the TV set.

It had been kind of him to offer her a lift, but really it would be dangerous to be cooped up with him in the car. It took a lot of effort to sit that close to him while having to remain aloof.

The thing was, Chrissy knew that if

107

she ever did fall in love, it would probably be with a man like Mark. And that scared her; she didn't want to give those feelings a chance to grow. Her best plan was to avoid him.

Mark was handsome, he was kind, and he was so talented it actually hurt her head to think about it. But weren't most men charming when you first got to know them? Her mother's many companions had been. But it hadn't taken any of them very long to show their true colours. Chrissy knew she'd save herself an awful lot of bother by concentrating on her career and forgetting romance.

★　★　★

'Have some breakfast, darling,' her mother urged the next morning as Chrissy picked up her jacket and shrugged it on. She was pleased to see her mum looking bright after her late night. Hopefully time with the girls had lifted her spirits. And hopefully, she hadn't met another man.

'Can't, Mum. Sorry.' She offered her mother a quick smile as she grabbed her bag.

'You have to eat,' she heard her mother shout just as she closed the door.

Yes, eating was important, but getting to the farm before Mark arrived to pick her up was suddenly the most vital thing in the world.

Once outside, she broke into a trot, but had only reached the end of the road when a car pulled up alongside. It seemed that however early her Sunday morning was starting, Mark's had begun even earlier.

She seriously considered refusing to get in. But she had no earthly reason for doing that — as far as he was concerned, they were friends. He had no idea of how she was starting to feel about him, or that she'd decided to give him a wide berth. And she was determined to keep it like that, because there was no need for him to know.

She pasted a smile on her face and went to get in. But when she sat down and looked into his face, the breath whooshed from her lungs, and the enforced grin was replaced with the real thing. His expression of surprise told her more clearly than any mirror that her smile was too much. For a moment she was stunned by her own reaction, and she could feel hot colour creeping up her chest and neck and to her face. Though she still couldn't stop smiling at him. And, slowly, his surprised expression was replaced by a smile of his own.

'You're out and about early,' she said when she eventually managed to stop grinning like an idiot.

'I've been to the café — Jack asked me drop off some of Mum's preserves from the larder. What's your excuse?'

'I wanted to get up to the farmhouse before you came to fetch me.' She could have bitten off her tongue — she hadn't wanted him to know that. She glanced across to find one eyebrow up to his fiery red hairline, though his eyes were still on the road. 'I didn't want to put you out,' she rushed to explain, glad he wasn't looking at her.

He grinned. 'You're not putting me out.' His voice was as soft as a caress, and a shiver ran down her spine. It was odd — he looked so like his brothers; but of the three, he stood out a mile for her. And when she was with him — and especially when he smiled at her — her heart beat a little faster, exactly as it was doing now. Which wasn't good.

Just for a moment, though, she did allow herself the indulgence of wondering what if . . . A pair of strong arms holding her tight, warm lips kissing her, and someone to care for her . . . It was all very seductive.

'Is there any news about Angus this morning?' she asked, both in an effort to get her mind back to the current situation, and because she was genuinely concerned.

It might have been her imagination, but it seemed as if Mark's body tensed at the mention of the other man. 'I spoke to Alexandra before I came into the village. She stayed at the farm last night, but she'd phoned the hospital first thing. Angus is apparently doing as well as can be expected.'

Chrissy breathed a loud sigh of relief. 'Thank goodness for that.'

Mark drove into the McGregor farmyard and stopped the car before turning to look at her. 'He still means a lot to you?'

She was a little surprised by his serious tone, so she shrugged. 'We've always been friends,' she said.

Luckily, her friendship with Angus had survived the romantic misunderstanding, but it wasn't a risk she wanted to take with Mark. She didn't want him to hate her when she had to tell him they weren't on the same page.

*   *   *

Mark wondered if he was ever going to manage to get any of his own work done. Keen to do the neighbourly thing and help a man who had been injured, he'd spoken to the farm hands that morning and offered his services on Angus's farm. They'd been so keen, they'd practically bitten his hand off.

'There's always a lot to do,' Joe had said. 'It might be Sunday, but work never stops on the farm, especially when there are animals to look after.'

And so it was settled.

Disappointingly, when he told Chrissy, she seemed quite relieved she was to have the place to herself that morning. 'Will you keep an eye out for Florence and Bob?' he asked. 'I don't want them trying to follow me over there.'

'I'll keep them in the office until you've headed out,' she assured him.

Once Chrissy and both dogs were safely settled, Mark got changed into his oldest jeans and top and headed over the fields for next door.

'This is so good of you,' Alexandra told him, the dark circles around her eyes telling him she'd barely slept.

Which was understandable — if it were one of his brothers who had been injured, Mark suspected he'd be in the same state.

'No problem,' he said, slightly embarrassed by her gratitude.

'I'm going to the hospital to see Angus in a minute,' she said. 'I know it's a bit early for visiting, but he looked pretty rough last night. Now they say he's more settled, I want to see for myself.'

Mark nodded. 'Just point me in the direction of what you need me to do.'

'Joe and Campbell know better than I do. They're in the barn, if you want to go and speak to them. I'll be back as soon as I can to lend a hand.'

Joe and Campbell set him to work immediately — moving bags of feed, and then helping with mending fences in the top field. Mark had never worked as hard in a physical sense outside of a gym. It was dangerous, because it left his mind free to think. And his empty mind filled itself with thoughts of

Chrissy: how cute she'd looked as she blushed that morning. How her scent had filled his car and stayed with him, and filled his imagination even now.

Before he knew it, he'd finished his assigned tasks, and was preparing to leave for the McGregors' farmhouse.

'Stay for lunch,' Alexandra urged, freshly back from the hospital, where she'd satisfied herself her brother had enjoyed a restful night.

'Kind of you to offer,' he said with a grin, 'but I'd better get back'. He might have accepted if it wasn't for the fact he knew Chrissy would be waiting for him.

At least he hoped she would be. He frowned as he made his way back across the field towards his temporary home. She might have gone home if she'd finished her work. The thought left him feeling bleak.

But he knew she was there as soon as he stepped over the threshold. There was a buzz about the place that was missing when she wasn't in. He popped his head into the office and couldn't help smiling as he saw her, deep in concentration and frowning at her computer screen.

'Busy morning?' he asked, and smiled again as she gave a little start. 'Sorry, didn't mean to startle you.'

'That's OK.' She grinned back at him and he stepped into the office and perched on the edge of her desk. 'I just didn't hear you come in, that's all.'

'Neither did they.' He nodded toward the floor near her chair at Florence and Bob, who both raised a lazy eye in his direction.

'How were things at the farm? I can't help feeling guilty that I didn't lend a hand, but there's so much still to do here.'

He shook his head and held up his hand to stop her. Nobody could fault her work ethic. 'You couldn't be in two places,' he told her. 'Besides, once word spreads I'm sure there'll be plenty of volunteers. Hopefully we'll all keep up the enthusiasm until Angus is on his feet again.'

She gave a little frown. 'Are you able to spare the time? It's not long now until your exhibition.'

'Don't remind me. But I'll have to make time. If there's one thing our parents drummed into us boys as we were growing up, it's that neighbours stick together.' She nodded. 'Do you have much more to do today?' he asked.

She glanced at all the papers littering her desk and grimaced. 'I'll be here another couple of hours.'

'OK — how about after I've had a shower, I rustle up some lunch, and you can take a bit of a break? I can make it up to you for that dinner we missed last night.'

She bit her lip and he knew she was going to refuse.

'You'll work twice as efficiently after you've refuelled.' He didn't dare to breathe as he waited for her verdict.

'OK,' she said at last. 'Lunch would be lovely. Thank you.'

He tried to be cool about it. He didn't want to scare her off by showing how much the thought of spending time with her mattered. 'Great.' He pushed himself up to standing and moved towards the door. 'I'll give you a shout when it's ready.'

10

Trusting Mark

Chrissy didn't know why having lunch with Mark was such a big deal, but it was. She made an effort to concentrate on her paperwork, but it was difficult. She was well accustomed now to seeing him in paint-splattered work clothes; but having him come to her office, glowing with vitality after a morning working in the fresh air, was quite another matter. He'd been deliciously dishevelled, his red hair pushed this way and that by impatient hands, his T-shirt torn where it had caught on something, affording her a glimpse of a well-developed bicep.

'Stop it,' she muttered under her breath. But it was no good; the image of him was firmly lodged in her mind.

It was almost a relief when he called

her to say lunch was ready. Being faced with the man himself had to be less of a torment than the pictures in her head. She followed the aroma of home cooking to the kitchen, to find a seafood lasagne on the table.

'One of Heather's?' she asked, thinking he must have taken it out of the freezer.

'Nope. All my own work.'

She was impressed, particularly when she sampled the first forkful.

'Well?' he asked. 'What do you think?'

'Delicious,' she told him without hesitation.

His answering grin had her heart fluttering in her chest. Her fork poised midway from her plate, she smiled shyly back. And something zinged its way between them as their eyes met. Something Chrissy knew she didn't want, but that made her heart soar nonetheless.

'I'll have to return the compliment and make something for you one of these days,' she said at last, in a desperate attempt to defuse the situation.

'I'd like that.' He smiled again.

And she wondered why she'd made the offer. It wasn't that she couldn't cook — you couldn't work in an office in Heather McGregor's home and not pick up some handy hints in the culinary department. But she certainly wasn't in his league in the kitchen. More to the point, she had only just decided she didn't want to give him the wrong impression, but now things seemed to be getting very cosy between them. Not only that, but she could just imagine her mother and Juliet jumping to all sorts of conclusions if she brought a man home for a meal.

She wondered if she should say something. She'd already told him she wasn't interested in a relationship. But she was fully aware that these cosy meals might be telling him something else entirely.

'What's the matter, Chrissy? Why have you gone all quiet on me?'

She looked into blue eyes that were bright with amusement. 'I haven't changed my mind, you know. I'm still only looking for a friend.' She knew she was running the risk of sounding daft — after all, maybe that was all he was looking for, too. But she needed to put things straight between them. More for herself than for him, because sitting here with him over this intimate Sunday lunch, she knew it would be easy for her to forget.

'I know. You said.' He frowned. 'I don't understand why you're telling me this again. Are you worried I'm going to pounce on you?'

No — she was worried she might be the one to pounce on him. That shocked her. Kissing him had been a pleasant experience, and she found herself wishing for a repeat performance.

She sighed, knowing that only the truth would do, no matter what conclusions he might reach. 'I'm starting to really like you way too much — and it's frightening the life out of me.'

He looked taken aback. Though, after a moment, he put down his knife and fork and reached across the table and took her hand. And she liked that way too much, too.

'Why does liking me frighten you?'

She wasn't sure she should tell him. It wasn't something she normally discussed with anybody. But this was Mark, and he wasn't just anybody. Even though something sizzled between them whenever they were together, it went beyond that. She knew instinctively that she could trust him with this secret — something she knew was so daft she hadn't dared to share it before. Maybe it was his sensitive artist's soul reaching out to her on a level she didn't quite understand. Whatever, it scared her.

'You know my dad died when Juliet and I were children.' He nodded. 'It was rough,' she told him. 'On all of us. We were all so miserable, especially Mum. She went a little bit off the rails, dating other men. And that was rough on us, too.'

She knew she should take her hand back, but it felt so right nestled in his.

What harm would it do to leave it there just a little longer? His thumbs began to move in hypnotic circles on the sensitive skin on the underside of her wrist, and she had to stifle a contented sigh.

'I never want to put a family of my own through something like that,' she said. 'So I decided years ago the only way to stop my husband dying was not to have one in the first place.'

He shook his head, his blue eyes troubled. 'That's not really a very rational argument.'

'My head knows that. But my heart . . .' She took her hand away from his at last and laid it over her chest. 'My heart is petrified of being hurt. Of falling in love. Of getting married. Of my husband dying and leaving me and any children we might have.'

He shook his head. 'Chrissy, that's not a normal way to think. You can't refuse to live your life just because you're worried someone might die.'

'It's not just that,' she admitted, knowing she had to tell him her deepest fear. That was something she'd never admitted to anyone — even though, going by her overheard conversation with Joyce, her mother had guessed. 'I'm worried I might be like my mother. What if my husband died and I spent the rest of my life chasing unsuitable men?'

'Do you think that's likely?'

'I hope not. But I just don't know.'

He reached for her hand again and grazed his lips across her fingers. 'I don't want to get married, either. I'm happy with my life the way it is.'

She smiled. 'That's what Angus said. And then it became awkward when he changed his mind. Men always seem to get the wrong idea around me, and it's easier just to keep away from relationships.'

'Not all men are like Angus.'

'There was Sam, too. He got the wrong end of the stick. And a boy I went out with at school. He wanted to get engaged when we were sixteen. I'd thought I was only helping him with his maths homework. He got pretty nasty when I turned him down.'

He was quiet for a moment, hating that there were men in the world who took it for granted a pretty girl would be receptive to — and grateful for, even — their advances. Some men even took it as their right, he knew, that a beautiful woman was there only for their entertainment. If those were the only experiences Chrissy had had with men, then coupled with her mother's history, it was no wonder she was running scared.

'How about I make you a promise?' he asked softly. 'If I swear by all I hold dear that I will never propose marriage to you, can we just see where this leads?'

She was finding it difficult to concentrate when he was so close; when the feel of his breath was still warm on her hand and he was working small circles on her wrist again. But somehow his suggestion sank in. She liked Mark. She loved spending time with him. This lifeline, where they could enjoy being together without any expectation of a commitment, seemed the answer to everything.

'I think, Mark McGregor, I might like that.'

He drew her to her feet and pulled her closer. 'To seal the deal,' he said as she settled into his arms and his lips descended toward hers.

'Much more suitable than a hand-shake,' she murmured against his kiss.

* * *

Mark's perfect Sunday afternoon with Chrissy was still on his mind as he wandered towards the farmhouse the next day. A lorry had been carelessly abandoned in the farmyard, its door lying open. Lorries, while not usually there at midday, had been known to come back if the driver had forgotten something. So he thought little of it. He'd had another busy morning at the farm and he was anticipating a long shower, then starting on his paintings.

It wasn't until Sam nearly knocked him off his feet in his rush to leave the house that Mark suspected there might be more to it than a driver's hurried return because of a missing load.

'Sorry,' Sam said, folding his arms and sounding anything but. 'That woman's driving me mad. You really need to do something about her.'

Mark felt his jaw clench. 'What woman?' Though there was only one woman he could be talking about.

'Chrissy.' Sam spat the name out and Mark immediately felt his hackles rise.

'What's the problem?' He was pleased his voice was calm and even. It wouldn't do to show how annoyed he was with Sam's tone.

'Giving orders like she owns the place,' Sam huffed.

'She is running the business at the moment,' Mark told him reasonably.

'Your dad said you were to be in charge. Why don't you act like it and sort her out?'

'What's the problem?'

'She wants me to drive into Aberbrig to collect a load. I've only just come back from there.'

'Making collections and deliveries is your job,' Mark told him. 'And Chrissy is in charge of the schedule.'

Sam sneered. 'Thought you'd take her side. Fancy your chances there, do you? Rather you than me, mate — that woman's nothing but trouble.'

Mark could feel his blood pressure rise. His fingers curled into tight fists and he had to keep his hands at his side so he wasn't tempted to thump Sam. 'I think you'd better stop there,' he said, a quiet warning in his tone. 'Now either you want to work here and you do as Chrissy asked you, or you decide you'd be better off elsewhere and go back to the office and resign.'

Sam harrumphed, but he walked to his lorry and got in. Mark was still simmering as he went to see if Chrissy was OK.

She seemed calm enough and was at her desk, speaking on the phone to a client about a delivery. She looked up as he walked in.

'You OK?' he mouthed.

She grinned and nodded. But he noticed her face was flushed, and it seemed the encounter with Sam had upset her. Rather than head straight for the shower as he'd planned, he sat down and waited for her to finish her call. Eventually she wound things up and replaced the receiver.

'I take it from your expression you've seen Sam?' she asked.

'I've seen Sam,' he said.

'And . . . ?'

'Does he often get like that?'

'He's full of bluster,' she told him. 'He sometimes goes complaining to your father, but Denny tells him my word's final when it comes to the schedule.'

Mark nodded. 'I told him the same.'

She smiled. 'Thanks. I thought you might, but there's always that moment of doubt when someone airs a grievance.'

'You're in charge of the business

while Dad's away, Chrissy. That's never in doubt.' He got to his feet. 'Does he make a habit of giving you a hard time?'

'Sometimes.' She shrugged. 'It's not a problem. I can handle it.'

'Does Dad know?'

There was a fierce light in her green eyes as she met his gaze and she lifted her chin. 'I can do my job, Mark. I don't need anyone to babysit me. When any of the drivers kick off, then I deal with them.'

He knew she was more than capable of doing her job, or his father would never have been happy to give her so much responsibility. But his protective instincts were going into overdrive, and the thought of anyone upsetting Chrissy was not a pleasant one. He could tell she wasn't pleased, though; her green eyes were practically fizzing and she was on her feet, too, now.

'I've no doubt you can handle the job,' he said, wanting to make things better between them. 'But he shouldn't be questioning your authority.'

She smiled then. 'Thank you for caring,' she said. 'But honestly, Mark, it's fine.'

He wasn't convinced, but she smiled again and he was suddenly unable to think straight.

'Now, tell me, what news is there of Angus?'

She wanted to know about Angus. Again. It was only natural, of course, that she would be interested. But he wished he didn't feel the twinges of . . . jealousy, it had to be, whenever he heard the other man's name on Chrissy's lips.

'Bearing up,' he said. 'The locals have set up a rota to help out, so I won't be needed as often from now on.' In theory, that would mean he might be able to finish his own work on time. If he could get Chrissy out of his head long enough to pick up a paint brush, that was.

11

Facing Facts

Chrissy arrived home that night to find a strange man on the doorstep and her mother dressed for another night out. 'This is Leonard,' she told her daughter with a smile as she grabbed the man's arm and pulled him towards a car Chrissy supposed must be his. And Chrissy's heart sank at the air of desperation that had her mother hanging on to the man's arm right until he deposited her to the passenger seat.

'It might not last,' Joyce's voice came over the garden fence as Chrissy watched them drive off. She grimaced, not at all soothed by this suggestion. A broken romance always led to great drama in her mother's world. And that meant Chrissy and Juliet would suffer, too.

'I just want her to be happy,' she said to her neighbour. 'And I don't think chasing after men she barely knows in an attempt to find a replacement for Dad is going to do it.'

Joyce cast her a sympathetic look. 'Do you have time for a cup of tea?'

Chrissy glanced at her watch. It was nearly seven, but it wasn't as though she had anything else to do. Besides, it was a long time since she'd had a nice chat with Joyce. 'I'd love that, thank you.'

Once she was seated in Joyce's cosy kitchen, a cup of tea safely in her hands, Chrissy managed to relax a little.

'She's always been like that, you know,' Joyce told her kindly. 'I've known her all her life, and ever since she was old enough to notice boys, she's been chasing after them.'

Chrissy's eyes widened in shock. Not only was it a surprise to hear Joyce speaking like this, but she'd never before given any thought to what her mother might have been like before she'd married.

'She did?'

Joyce nodded. 'Your mother is one of those women who's always needed a man's company. She doesn't feel validated unless she has a partner.'

Chrissy took a sip of her tea. It had never crossed her mind that that had been the case. 'I always thought she was trying to replace Dad — that she'd loved him so much she couldn't face life without that kind of relationship.'

'Maybe that has influenced her a little,' Joyce admitted. 'She and your father were very lucky to have found each other. They were completely in love, nobody could doubt that.'

'But you're saying she had a lot of boyfriends before.' Chrissy could barely believe it — and yet, now Joyce had brought the subject up, it did make an odd kind of sense.

Joyce nodded. 'It was much the same pattern as now. She'd meet someone, they'd show a bit of interest, and in her mind she'd already moved on to the happily-ever-after. Even though most of them were hugely unsuitable.'

Chrissy frowned. Joyce was right; it was a pattern. A pattern it seemed her mother had entered into in young adulthood and had reverted to once her happy marriage had ended with the death of a much-loved spouse.

'You're nothing like her, you know. If that's what's worrying you.'

Chrissy felt her face flush. This all felt horribly disloyal to her mother — yet she still needed to have this conversation with Joyce. She needed to understand — to get her own head around the fact — that for all these years she'd been wrong. Her mother wasn't dating all these men because she was trying to recreate a happy marriage; she was doing it because she couldn't help it. It was in her DNA to chase after men. And it was only meeting Chrissy's father that had paused that pattern for a while. This was who her mum was — who she'd always been. And the loyal, demure wife had only been a part of her personality.

But Chrissy grasped at the glimmer of hope that Joyce offered her. 'How can you be so sure I'm not like her?'

Joyce laughed. 'Oh my dear girl, how can you even ask me that? Just the fact you're worried about it proves you're not.'

'How do you know I'm worried?'

Joyce put her cup and saucer very carefully onto the kitchen table. 'I didn't think you were until recently. But now I've seen the way you look at young Mark McGregor.' Chrissy opened her mouth to deny there was anything between them, but Joyce raised her hand. 'And I've seen the way he looks at you. When the two of you think there's nobody taking any notice, your behaviour is quite revealing. Yet you both dance around the issue.'

Chrissy felt her cheeks grow warm. 'What way . . . what way does he look at me?' Yes, he flirted with her; yes, there'd been kissing. But as for anything else . . .

'It looks to me very much like he's mad about you.'

She wanted to believe what Joyce was telling her, but she didn't know if she dared.

'And the fact that you're still adamant you're having nothing to do with him,' Joyce continued, 'very much suggests you're scared.'

It was too much for Chrissy. Even though it was no more than she'd deduced for herself, and however much she liked and respected Joyce, she couldn't listen to this. 'I'm fine as I am,' she insisted, more for her own benefit than anything else. 'I have the job I always wanted and I'm taking on more responsibility there. I have no time for a man.'

Joyce gave a short nod and gathered the now-empty teacups and put them in the sink. 'As long as you know what you're doing,' she said briskly, 'and are prepared to live with the consequences.'

'You're OK on your own, aren't you?' Chrissy asked quietly as the other woman rinsed the cups.

'I'm absolutely OK, yes.' She came over and sat back down. 'I've lived life on my own terms; had a career I loved. And now I have a home I paid for with my own hard work, and a decent pension. But if I'd met someone . . . ' She paused, her expression a little shocked — almost as though she was surprised she'd given so much away to a woman who she'd always treated as the child from next door.

'If you'd met someone — ?' Chrissy prompted softly.

Joyce sighed. 'If I'd met someone special, things might have been different. I might have married; had a family. And those things are important, too.'

Chrissy frowned. 'I don't understand. If you're happy as you are, then why do you regret not getting married?'

'I'm content,' Joyce corrected. 'And I don't regret my single life. But sometimes I do think how things would have been if I'd a husband and children. I might even have had grandchildren by now.'

Chrissy reached a tentative hand out to rest on Joyce's arm. Joyce wasn't the touchy-feely type, so she didn't know if the contact would be welcome. But when the other woman didn't object, Chrissy squeezed her hand in a gesture of support.

'If you've met someone special,' Joyce continued, 'then please don't let him go because you're scared. If you do, you may regret it one day.'

* * *

Mark's habit when working was to cut all other distractions from his mind. But tonight — again — he hadn't been able to think of anything apart from Chrissy. As he worked well into the night, he could tell that his preoccupation showed in his unimaginative use of colour, and in his lack of light and shade. And even if everything was all in the right place, it just wasn't *right*.

When Chrissy appeared in the barn many hours after she'd left to go home, he thought at first he'd conjured her up. After all, he hadn't heard a car arrive — but then, he had been engrossed in his own thoughts.

He blinked, but she was still there, standing in the doorway, looking hesitant. And that was when he began to hope that maybe he'd been on her mind as much as she'd been on his that evening.

'I know it's late, but I had to get away,' she said.

He glanced at his watch. 'It's nearly midnight.'

'I know, but is it OK if I stay with you for a while?'

She looked shattered. Her already pale skin had taken on a grey sheen — she looked almost translucent. Her normally rosebud-pink lips had turned nearly white.

Without thinking, he dropped his paintbrush and held his arms out towards her. With a sigh, she stepped towards him, her own arms going up around his waist. He held her tight and relished the feel of her slender arms holding him. The fragrance from her shampoo teased his nose, and he sighed against her hair.

'Do you want to talk about it?'

She shook her head. 'No,' she said. 'Just hold me for a moment, please.'

He didn't know how long they stood there, but he was content with her in his arms and didn't feel inclined to move. But eventually she pulled away slightly and looked up into his eyes.

'Thanks,' she said. Her green eyes were huge, but the colour was coming back to her cheeks. And she was smiling.

'You're very welcome.' It seemed the most natural thing in the world to dip his head and brush her lips with his. The effect was electrifying. As he lifted his head away, her lips parted, her gaze fixed on his mouth. The invitation was too much to resist.

Their previous kiss couldn't have prepared either of them for this one. She moulded herself against him, standing so close he could feel her heart beating against his chest and his arms closed around her, gathering her even nearer. As she kissed him back, he reached up and undid her ponytail, allowing her red hair to fill his hands. On some level he suspected he should stop this now, but when she tasted so good and felt so right in his arms it was difficult to think. Slowly, as they kissed, her hands roamed beneath his shirt to stroke the bare skin on his back. And he'd never felt so close to her.

'Chrissy.' Her name was a whisper as he pulled away. The colour had come back to her lips now and he smiled, knowing it was his kiss that had done it. 'I think we should go into the house. It's getting chilly out here and I don't want you getting cold.'

She nodded and allowed him to lead her by the hand towards the warmth of the farmhouse.

'I didn't know who else to go to,' she admitted once they were in Heather McGregor's large kitchen. The heat from the Aga reached out to them and they both gravitated towards it.

He nodded. 'I'm glad you felt you could come here.'

'I've always felt safe here,' she admitted. 'When I was small, Dad used to bring me to work here with him. Do you remember?'

He did. As a child he'd been quiet, not like his brothers at all, and he'd kept away from the noisy little red-haired tomboy Chrissy had been in those days. Jack had been a good few years older, but she'd been good friends with Ryan. But Mark did remember her. And he remembered being fascinated by her energy and her love of life.

'I think that's why I love this place so much,' she said. 'On some level, even though I don't want to remember, the farm reminds me of him.'

'What happened to upset you tonight?'

She sighed. 'I shouldn't be talking about this. I mean, it's not about me. But my mother went out on a date tonight and she seemed so happy when she left.'

'That's good, isn't it?'

'Not really. She's always happy at first. But what if this guy is just another in a long line of disasters?'

He was quiet for a moment. 'You can't know he will be.'

'Going by her history, it doesn't look good — and I don't want to see her crying over a man again.'

He sighed. He wasn't equipped to deal with this. And it was none of Mark's business — apart from the fact that it is upsetting Chrissy, and that fact alone was enough to make him want to help. 'Have you tried speaking to her? Telling her how you feel?'

Chrissy nodded. 'I can't understand it. She's a strong woman in so many ways, but she has this weakness where unsuitable men are concerned.'

'It's her decision. She's an adult,' he told her quietly.

'I know. I just wish she could be happy being single.'

'Being alone isn't for everyone.' He met her gaze, and suddenly he wasn't talking about her mother any longer. This was about him — about the fact that when he looked into Chrissy's eyes, he knew exactly what he'd been missing all these years by refusing to settle down.

The air between them sizzled. And then, with a sigh, she was on her feet.

'I should be going,' she said, glancing at the clock. 'It's really late.'

'You could stay here,' he offered. For a moment there was silence. He could hear the beating of his own heart as he looked at her. 'With me.'

More silence. He held his breath. He couldn't believe her answer meant so much.

Her lips parted as she looked at him. For a moment it looked as though she might accept. But then she shook her head. 'Thanks, but I'd better get back. I don't have a change of clothes here for work tomorrow. Besides, Mum will be worried if she wakes up in the morning and I'm not there.'

'I'll drive you home.' He didn't like

the thought of her driving along the winding country roads back to the village on her own at this early hour of the morning.

There was a flash in her green eyes. She was about to assert her independence again, he could tell. And it could go either way. But then she smiled and he let out a sigh of relief that he hadn't annoyed her again by being overprotective. He knew she was able to look after herself, though that didn't mean he didn't want to make sure she was safe.

'I'll be fine,' she said. 'If it makes you feel better I'll text you when I get in.'

★   ★   ★

Chrissy had nearly agreed to stay. It was only the fact her mother and sister would find her missing in the morning that had stopped her. But she was smiling softly at the memory of Mark's kiss as she reached over to her bedside cabinet and picked up her phone. It seemed impossibly intimate to be texting Mark when she was tucked up cosily beneath her duvet. She should have done it before getting into her pyjamas and going to bed. But she'd delayed the moment, wanting to savour the anticipation of one last contact.

She tapped the message quickly: 'Home. Safe. Thanks for listening. See you tomorrow.'

He must have been waiting to hear from her, because her phone bleeped just a moment later: 'Pleasure. Sweet dreams.'

She drifted off to sleep with the phone tucked under her pillow and a smile on her face.

12

An Invitation

Considering how late her night had been, Chrissy was surprisingly upbeat the next morning as she got her bag and jacket together, ready for work. She drank the last of her coffee and took her cup over to rinse at the sink.

Her mother joined her in the kitchen and poured herself some cereal. 'You were out when I got home last night.'

Chrissy glanced up. Surprisingly, her mother was smiling — no sign of the high drama that normally accompanied the aftermath of one of her dates. 'There was something I needed to see to at work.' Her mother didn't need to know that the something was Mark, or that she'd needed to offload her worries onto him. 'Did you sleep well?'

Louise nodded. 'Better than I expected

to. I hope you're going to eat something before you go.'

'I'll pick a muffin up at the café on my way.'

Her mum looked as though she was about to preach the virtues of starting the day with a good breakfast, and Chrissy braced herself.

'OK,' Louise said at last. 'Just make sure you do. You can't work a full day on an empty stomach.'

Chrissy nodded, as she did every time her mum voiced a similar concern — but glad today was the abridged version. Though still the issue of her mother's desperate need for companionship worried her. She only wished Louise could be happy standing on her own feet emotionally, as she'd been doing financially for years. Chrissy knew Mark had been right, though — it wasn't her place to put any kind of pressure on her mum. But one question burned in her head until, with her hand on the door, it burst forth.

'How was your date with Leonard?'

Louise sighed. 'Don't be angry with me, Chrissy, but I'm going to see him again.'

'I'm not angry.' Chrissy hoped the fact her mother was happy that morning was a good sign. 'Can I ask you one thing, though, Mum?'

Louise paused with her spoonful of cereal halfway to her mouth and sent a quizzical look winging Chrissy's way.

'Take it one date at a time?' Chrissy unlatched the back door, needing to escape before she said too much.

'Don't worry about me,' her mum said, putting down her spoon and getting up from the table.

'You're my mum — of course I'm worried about you. I don't want you getting hurt again.'

'I'm tougher than I look.' Louise walked over and straightened the lapels of Chrissy's jacket, just as she'd done when Chrissy had been a little girl wearing a school blazer.

Chrissy sighed. 'You always do this — get your hopes up.'

'But if there's no hope, then what's the point?'

The concept was ridiculously simple, but that was when Chrissy finally understood: the heartache of the broken romances was worth it for her mother because if she found happiness in the end, then it would have been worth it.

'Have a good day, sweetheart,' Louise said as she give Chrissy a quick hug.

Chrissy sighed as she made her way outside. Her mother had cried so many tears over the past few years. Was it any wonder Chrissy shied away from giving her heart to a man? But maybe, just maybe, if she did let someone underneath her armour, she might find the risk worth it, too. If she was ever able to let go of her fears and the self-conditioning of a lifetime, that was.

★ ★ ★

The drivers were waiting in the yard when Chrissy arrived. After she'd spoken to them, they left with a roar of loud engine noise. She watched the last of them trundle down the farm track, and as she turned something caught her eye: Mark, making his way back from the farm next door.

She stood rooted to the spot, unable to take her eyes from him. As he got closer, she could see his eyes were fixed on her, too. He was deliciously dishevelled again, and just looking at him made her heart leap.

He stopped only feet away, and it was difficult to think straight when he was so close, messing with her head. 'Any news about Angus?' Her voice was a little breathless, but if he noticed he didn't react.

'Alexandra says he's doing well.'

'Oh, that's great news.' She smiled.

As she looked at him, he took a step towards her and his smile slipped a little. She got the distinct impression he was about to say something.

'What is it?' she asked when he didn't speak.

He ran a hand through his red hair. She'd never seen him look so gorgeous — and the prospect of letting her guard down had never seemed so enticing.

'My exhibition,' he said, and he was suddenly so uncertain that her heart went out to him. 'I wondered if you'd come with me to the opening?'

Chrissy didn't know what to say. She wanted to go, wanted to be with Mark, of course she did. But the thought of going to such a glittering event, especially one so important to his career, frightened the living daylights out of her. She might be happy with who she'd grown into, but sophisticated she was not — so how could she even begin to compete with the glamorous people who would be there?

'Mark . . . ' She faltered. 'I don't know.' As she looked up into his blue eyes and stared at his handsome face, she knew a strength she hadn't realised she possessed. Suddenly, she felt she could do anything — even take risks with her heart; and her fear dissolved.

Her lips parted and she exhaled a tiny breath. 'Actually, I think I'd like that.'

His slow grin made her knees weak. And she knew beyond doubt that she'd made the right decision.

'Great,' he said. And for a moment he stood and stared at her.

She thought he might step closer and kiss her. She wanted him to kiss her.

Instead, he ran his hand through his hair again and took a step back. 'I'd better get into the shower,' he said — and then he was gone.

★   ★   ★

Mark couldn't quite believe that he'd asked Chissy to the exhibition. He didn't make a habit of taking company: as a rule, he battled through these events alone. His family — even while his brothers were supportive of his career choice — had no interest in art. And as for the women who hung around, well, he had no interest in giving them the wrong idea by taking any of them to something that was so much a part of who he was.

His exhibitions were important to him. And so was Chrissy. Attending on his own seemed empty and pointless: he wanted her there by his side. He wanted to be able to hold her hand — and to show her off. And he wanted her to be proud of him.

He stepped under the shower's jet and closed his eyes.

He didn't know when it had happened, or how. But it seemed he was crazy about Chrissy. He didn't imagine she'd be best pleased when she found out.

He spent the rest of the morning in the barn, stopping only when Chrissy brought sandwiches in at lunchtime.

'It's looking good,' she said, nodding towards the seascape he'd been working on.

'Should get it finished this afternoon,' he said as he bit into a ham sandwich. 'I didn't expect you to bring me lunch.'

She smiled. 'You've fed me often enough. And you've been so engrossed in your work, I imagined you missing lunch completely.'

He was touched she'd thought of him, particularly as he knew she must be very busy herself. 'When I'm done here, how about we go for a walk down by the river? Clear some of the cobwebs away?'

'OK.' She nodded.

'Great. I'll call by the office in a couple of hours.'

His mind wasn't on his work — all he could think of was Chrissy. Which wasn't brilliant when his deadline was looming, and he'd already lost so much time with moving in here and spending time helping out next door.

He pushed on as best he could. When he deemed it was a respectable time for Chrissy to stop work for the day, he made his way towards the office.

As he walked into the farmhouse, the shouting reached him. Bob and Florence by his heels began to bark, and Mark broke into a run.

The argument was happening in the office. Mark felt a sudden surge of adrenaline as he thought that somebody might be raising their voice to Chrissy.

Sam. He had to stop himself biting out the name out loud as he saw the man looming over where Chrissy sat at her desk.

'Just admit it!' Sam shouted, his face getting redder and redder. 'I know it was you. You just can't stop yourself from causing trouble, can you?'

Chrissy's glare at the angry man was scathing. 'Nothing to do with me. Not that it wouldn't serve you right if I had told her.'

Sam took another step towards her, using his size and the fact he was on his feet and she was seated to intimidate her. Not that she looked intimidated; but beneath the feisty exterior, Mark suspected she might not be as cool as she seemed.

'What do you think you're doing?' he asked. If he hadn't been so angry, he might have laughed at the shocked expression on Sam's face as he turned. 'What's going on?' he persisted when the other man didn't answer. Mark was pleased by the quiet menace he heard in his own voice, and took a great deal of satisfaction from watching the overblown red drain from Sam's face, leaving him pale.

'None of your business, pal,' Sam snarled. 'Why don't you trot off to your crayons and leave me and Chrissy to sort this out between us.'

Yeah, right. Like he'd leave on Sam's say so. 'Chrissy?'

'It's OK, Mark.' Chrissy still didn't look in the least concerned. 'Sam was just leaving.'

Sam, though, didn't move, and Mark was forced to take a warning step towards him.

'Oh, all right, then.' Sam had obviously thought it wise not to tangle with Mark. It was clear he preferred to bully people much smaller than himself.

Mark stood aside to allow Sam to

leave the room, glaring at the other man for good measure. Then he turned towards Chrissy. 'Are you OK?'

'Fine.'

She wasn't happy; he could see she wasn't. And, from the way she frowned, it seemed her annoyance was directed at him rather than Sam. He'd encroached on her territory.

'I had to intervene, Chrissy,' he told her softly, stepping further into the office and sitting down so he was on the same level as she.

'I could have dealt with it,' she insisted, her green eyes bright. 'I *was* dealing with it.'

'From where I was standing, it looked as though things could have got nasty.'

'He's just a big bully. He likes to shout and make a fuss, but when someone stands up to him he soon backs down.'

Mark felt his muscles tense. He loathed bullies in any form. And he especially loathed that Chrissy had been subjected to this man's angry outburst.

'You should have called me,' he said.

'At the first sign of trouble, you should have picked up the phone and called me in.'

'And if I'd been out of my depth I would have. But I've known Sam a long time and I've dealt with his tantrums before.' She got to her feet and paced to the window, where she stood with her back towards him. He could see she was agitated and he didn't quite know what to do. Feeling helpless, he got to his feet and took a couple of uncertain steps towards her.

'Chrissy?'

She spun around and he was suddenly looking into the full glare of angry green eyes. Even though he knew he'd do the same again in a heartbeat, he also knew she deserved an apology.

'I'm sorry. I shouldn't interfere unless you ask me to.'

'No,' she agreed, 'you shouldn't.'

He gave a helpless shrug. 'But anything could have happened.'

'You stayed out of it when Sam complained to you about me,' she reminded him. 'And I appreciated that you trusted me enough to do that.'

'Last time I didn't catch him shouting at you and using threatening body language.'

Chrissy smiled. That shocked him. Disarmed him. Suddenly he didn't feel like arguing with her any longer.

'What . . . ' He was perplexed: who smiled in the middle of a disagreement? Who smiled when they'd just been subjected to an angry tantrum by a driver who was supposed to listen to orders?

'You're rather attractive when you're angry,' she said.

He couldn't help smiling back at her. Though he was still furious with Sam. 'Don't change the subject. That man needs to be sacked.'

'He's already had a written warning from your dad for trying to pick a fight with another driver a while back.'

'He needs another warning for today.' He propelled Chrissy back to her chair. 'Sit down,' he instructed. 'I'll go and make some tea.'

Over hot, sweet tea — which she insisted she didn't need — he gently insisted she tell him exactly what had happened to start Sam's tirade.

'His girlfriend dumped him,' she said. 'And he blames me.'

Mark frowned at her from across the desk. 'What can that possibly have to do with you?'

'She heard I threw my drink over him. She seems to think there might have been something between us. And he thinks I told her.'

Every single thing that Mark found out about this man was showing him in an increasingly unflattering light. Unable to help himself, he reached out and touched Chrissy's hand. Her fingers curled instantly around his.

'So who might have stirred things up with Sam's girlfriend?' Would anyone want to create trouble for you?'

'Not for me.' She shook her head. 'It will have been one of the guys, probably someone he's fallen out with.'

'Do you want me to ask some questions when they come in tomorrow?'

She shook her head. 'No need. I meant it when I said I can handle things.'

'OK.' He raised his free hand and let his fingers graze her cheek. 'In that case, how about we go for that walk now, while the sun's still shining?'

13

Falling for Mark

Chrissy didn't dwell on the Sam incident, but she couldn't pretend she was overly sorry when he didn't turn up for work over the next few days.

'I heard he was on holiday,' Juliet told her when she mentioned it over dinner one evening. 'Joyce told me.'

'He's supposed to be working. I've had to handle his deliveries the past few days.'

It seemed he'd resigned, if what Joyce had told Juliet was true. That was fine with Chrissy, though she'd have to rearrange the workload; she was way behind with the paperwork and it would be impossible to spend any more time out of the office.

'Come and help me with the washing-up,' she told her younger sister as she got up from the table. It was just the two of them, as their mother was out with Leonard again.

As Juliet rinsed a plate and handed it to Chrissy for drying, her nose wrinkled. 'So, do you want to tell me what's going on with you and Mark McGregor?'

The cup Chrissy was drying nearly fell from her fingers. 'What do you mean?' she asked, knowing full well exactly what her sister wanted to know, but playing for time so she could think of how to answer.

'It seems to me,' Juliet said as she gave the serving bowl she was washing a particularly thorough scrub, 'that there might be something in the air there.' She turned her head to give Chrissy a long, inquisitive look.

Chrissy knew she should deny that there was something going on between herself and Mark. After all, there wasn't. But she didn't want to. She couldn't bear the thought of meaning nothing to him.

In that moment she realised she'd

somehow fallen for Mark in a big way. Despite her lifelong belief she could stop something like this happening, and despite wanting to remain in control of her heart, it had somehow crept up on her.

'Just get on with washing up,' she told her sister. 'The sooner we get it done, the sooner we can relax.'

Juliet's soft laughter proved she wasn't convinced. It was just as well Chrissy hadn't told her sister about the invitation to Mark's exhibition. Juliet would have added two and two and come up with a hundred and twenty over that.

* * *

Paula and Vicky were deep in conversation when Chrissy went into the café. She had it in mind to buy some cake to take up to the farm; it was good manners to return a favour when a friend had fed you as many times as Mark had fed her.

'What's up?' she asked the two as she approached the counter.

'We're just talking about the wedding,' Vicky shared, grinning widely. 'I've already got my dress, and Jess's bridesmaid's dress is all sorted,' she explained, mentioning Paula's stepdaughter. 'But I still need to sort out the matron of honour's outfit — and Paula was wondering what to wear.'

'I have plenty of outfits, but they'll be a bit tight by the time the date arrives.' Paula smiled as she patted her pregnant tummy. 'I think I'm going to have to take a trip into the city. Shall we make it a girls' outing? The morning sickness has eased up, but I know Jack will still fuss if I go on my own.'

'Well I don't see why I can't come with you,' Vicky said. 'We can make a weekend of it — it can be my hen weekend. I'll get Claire to come along, too.'

Paula's grin showed she thought it was a good plan, but she still seemed a little hesitant. 'Do you want to go maternity dress shopping on your hen do?' she asked.

'I can't think of anything that would be more fun,' Vicky told her. 'We can all buy something new. The shops in Aberbrig are perfectly adequate, but the chance to shop in the city should never be turned down. Isn't that right?' she asked Chrissy.

Chrissy nodded. She wasn't one for shopping, but she knew she'd have to make a trip into the city herself soon, if she was going to go to Mark's exhibition. It wasn't just one of those things women said: she really didn't have anything remotely suitable to wear.

'And you should come, too,' Vicky said, looking at Chrissy.

She was sure she must have misunderstood, but Vicky and Paula continued to look expectantly in her direction. 'Oh, I couldn't possibly intrude,' she said at last.

'Don't be silly,' Vicky said with a smile. 'You're practically one of the family. How could you intrude?'

Chrissy felt her face flush. To be included along with Vicky's sister Claire and her soon-to-be sister-in-law Paula seemed a little overwhelming. And, even though Heather McGregor had often made a similar comment — and even though Chrissy knew it was only because of the time she spent working at the farmhouse — it still made her glow with pleasure.

'Actually,' Chrissy started, knowing it would seem she was doing a massive u-turn, 'I do need a new outfit. Mark's asked me to go to his exhibition, and I don't have anything remotely suitable.'

Vicky and Paula exchanged glances.

'What is it?' Chrissy asked, suspecting she'd said the wrong thing.

'Mark never invites anyone to those events,' Paula told her. 'Jack was only saying the other day.' Her face broke into a grin. 'Do you know what that means?'

'I think Mark McGregor might have found himself a girlfriend,' Vicky joined in the good-natured teasing.

'No,' Chrissy denied, her face burning. 'It's nothing like that.

The other two smiled, not unkindly. 'Shame,' Paula said. 'You'd fit right in with us.'

And Chrissy rather thought she might — if that had been the kind of life she wanted. But she wanted to be master of her own destiny; she wanted to be in charge of her own life and keep things on an even keel with no nasty surprises. Besides, however she felt about him, Mark had told her he wasn't interested in anything serious.

'A weekend away does sound good, though,' she said, attempting to deflect the conversation.

Vicky grinned. 'Good, lets sort out dates and I'll book us some hotel rooms.'

*　*　*

'Angus is looking much better.' Mark was sitting on the edge of her desk when she arrived, arms crossed against his chest and long legs stretched out in front of him.

'Brilliant news.' Chrissy still couldn't get over how horrible the accident had been, but she was so relieved Angus was OK now.

'It will take him a while before he's back to full strength, but Lexi's set up a rota of willing helpers. So that means my farm boy days are over.'

'A good thing, too,' Chrissy told him, though she secretly thought she'd rather miss the sight of him arriving back at the McGregors' after a morning's hard physical labour. 'It will give you time to work on your paintings for the exhibition.'

He ran a hand roughly through his red hair and grimaced.

'There's a lot to do.'

'I know.' She felt a little guilty that she'd distracted him so often. 'I've brought some cake from Paula's, for us to have with our morning cuppa,' she told him — as though that would make it better.

'Great. Though now Mum's away, I

think Jack's been helping in the baking department.'

Chrissy smiled, knowing Heather had taught her three sons the way around a kitchen. She was sure the cake she'd bought would be lovely.

'When I was there, Vicky invited me along on her hen weekend.'

'And what did you say?'

'It would have been rude to refuse.'

'Don't you want to go?'

Chrissy gave an easy shrug. 'I just feel I don't belong there. I don't know Vicky very well and I don't want to be in the way.'

'Vicky wouldn't have asked if she didn't want you to go.'

'I know.' She sat at her desk and switched her computer on. 'I'm being silly.'

'Naw.' He shook his head. 'But you have to remember that Vicky was working away for a long time; she's probably lost touch with most of her old friends and she'll be trying to make new ones. She'll be pleased to have you there.'

Chrissy thought about that as she worked on the accounts after Mark had gone off to his makeshift studio. She still didn't quite know how it had happened that she'd been invited along on Vicky's hen weekend. She was looking forward to it, though — even if it all did seem a bit too cosy.

★   ★   ★

Mark couldn't decide how he felt about Chrissy joining Paula and Vicky on this weekend away. Of course it was none of his business, but he would miss her, he knew. On the other hand, it boded well: it seemed she'd already been accepted by both his brothers' partners; something she seemed to welcome. She was already fitting seamlessly into his family.

No — he stopped himself thinking that way. Not so long ago she'd disliked him enough to cause a fuss because he was going to be staying here. He'd sworn to win her over; to become her friend. He'd done that — and he had to be satisfied. If anything else was to happen, then it would have to be instigated by Chrissy.

Predictably, Mark couldn't keep his mind on his work. This was becoming something of a habit. And he knew the reason: she was sitting in the office of his father's haulage company, merrily getting on with her work.

She was a cool customer. Even though they had shared some pretty explosive kisses, and even though she'd agreed to go to his exhibition, Chrissy wasn't giving anything away about how she was feeling. Which maybe was an indicator that she wasn't feeling anything at all. Though she did smile at him more than she used to. That had to be a good thing, didn't it?

He made a huge effort to concentrate and, in the end, got more done than he'd expected. When his stomach rumbled and indicated it was maybe time for a break, he went through to the kitchen to put the kettle on, looking forward to seeing Chrissy.

It worried him how much he was looking forward to seeing her. Even more worrying, he wasn't looking forward to going back to his own place — which was a shame, as his parents would be home soon and things would have to go back to normal.

Chrissy came into the kitchen. 'How did you get on this morning?' she asked.

'Good, thanks.' Mark smiled and was rewarded with the same in return. Yes, she was definitely smiling more these days. 'How about you?'

'I officially hate accounts.' She wrinkled her nose. 'But they have to be done.'

They sat down and he poured tea for them both from his mother's teapot, while she served the cake she'd bought at the café onto plates — large slices of Victoria sponge, he noticed with a smile. His brother Jack didn't have an adventurous streak when it came to baking, but the simple cakes he made were good.

'Have you seen anything of Sam?' he asked, making the question sound casual, even though he was prepared to deal with the man if he'd caused Chrissy any more problems.

'No.' She shook her head. 'I heard he's not been seen in the village for a while. Some say he's gone on holiday, but I'm hoping he's left for good.'

'Well, if he does come back, and if he says anything at all out of place, let me know.'

She reached out across the scrubbed kitchen table and covered his hand with her own. The shock of her touch made his breath catch and he turned his hand so their palms touched. And he looked into green eyes and tried to see what she might be thinking.

'That's very sweet,' she told him. 'But not necessary. I've told you.'

His fingers tightened around hers. 'Just because you can take care of yourself, doesn't mean you should always have to.'

She sighed. 'You're not going to be around much longer,' she told him. 'I'd rather not get used to you sticking up for me.'

'Well that's going to be rather a problem, because I can't seem to help it.'

She didn't say anything, but a green flash of annoyance met his steady gaze.

'Put yourself in my shoes,' he urged. 'If you saw someone giving me a hard time, wouldn't you be tempted to intervene?'

'Of course I would.' Her answer came without hesitation. Then she seemed flustered. 'It's what friends do,' she said, almost as though she was trying to explain to herself why she'd come up with that very definite response.

'Yes,' he agreed. 'Friends look out for each other.'

And so do lovers, he finished silently — because he knew that was just the kind of sentimental nonsense Chrissy Grieves wasn't interested in.

Despite the fact she was holding his hand just as tightly as he was holding hers.

14

A Girls' Weekend

For all that Chrissy had spent the run up being hesitant about joining in with Vicky's hen do, once they were all on the train she actually started to relax and enjoy herself. Spirits were high. And the laughing and joking carried on to the hotel, where Vicky had booked rooms for them all.

Paula was sharing with her teenage step-daughter, Jess, but Vicky had pushed the boat out and everyone else had their own rooms.

'This is lovely,' Chrissy said as she threw herself onto the bed. With money having been scarce, she'd barely had the chance to stay in a hotel while she'd been growing up. And once she'd started working, she hadn't been in the habit of spoiling herself that way.

Holidays at her grandfather's had been what she and Juliet had come to expect.

Vicky laughed; she'd insisted on a look at all the rooms to ensure they were up to scratch. 'It's a bit extravagant, but this is once in a lifetime for me, so I'm quite happy to foot the bill,' she said.

Chrissy was appalled. 'I'll be paying my own bill,' she insisted. 'I'm very pleased to be here, but you've got a wedding to pay for and a new home to set up.'

Vicky, hand on hips, frowned. 'We'll see,' she said.

But Chrissy had already made up her mind and she wouldn't be dissuaded.

They hit the shops as soon as they could.

'Do you have an outfit for the wedding?' Vicky's sister Claire asked Chrissy as they walked along behind the others.

'I do,' Chrissy said, smiling. She was pleased she was going to get a chance to wear her pretty lilac dress at last. She'd bought it in the sales a couple of years ago, but had long thought it a false economy, because she hadn't had a chance to wear it yet. The weather had been too cold when Jack and Paula had married. And it wasn't sophisticated enough to wear to Mark's exhibition. Vicky and Ryan's wedding would give it the perfect outing. 'What about you?'

'I'm hoping to find my matron of honour dress this weekend,' she confided. 'I've plenty of clothes that might do, but it's not every day your sister gets married, and I feel I deserve a treat.'

And Chrissy agreed. Claire had been through a difficult time recently. Her husband, a roofer, had fallen and been badly hurt. He'd only recently been able to go back to work after a long convalescence.

'I am hoping to buy something special,' though, Chrissy confided in Claire and she told her about the invitation to the opening of Mark's new exhibition.

'Oh, that will be a glamorous occasion.'

Claire wasn't telling her anything she didn't know, but still a feeling dread crept over Chrissy. She was so desperate not to let Mark down. 'That's what worries me,' she said. 'I think I'm going to be well out of my depth.'

Claire shook her head. 'Mark wouldn't have invited you unless he thought you'd be able to cope.'

Mildly reassured, Chrissy resolved to put her worries from her mind and concentrate on one thing at a time. After all, she'd been concerned about this weekend and she was enjoying herself already.

They went from boutique to boutique, each picking up the bits they'd been looking for, and some they hadn't. Shopping had never been high on Chrissy's list of priorities, but she felt she held her own on this trip. What was more, she was actually loving it. The company helped, of course, but it was looking for something special to wear for Mark that made this so much more than just an ordinary expedition.

Chrissy's feet were aching by the time she got back to her room. She kicked off her shoes and lay back on the bed on top of the cover. She wondered what Mark was doing now. She pictured him in the barn, a frown on his face as he concentrated on light and shade and colours.

Her phone was in her hand. It would be so easy to ring him; to hear his voice. But what would she say? He'd think her an idiot if she rang without an excuse. Dare she?

A light tapping at her door made the decision for her; it was Vicky. 'Come and join us,' she urged. 'We're hanging out in Paula and Jess's room — it's bigger than the others.'

'OK.' Chrissy smiled as she slipped her shoes back on and followed Vicky down the hall.

'We thought about going to the restaurant for dinner,' Vicky told her, 'but it might be more fun to order room service and watch a romcom.'

Chrissy liked the sound of that plan.

In fact, she liked this entire family. It made her sad that she was an outsider. If only things could have been different between her and Mark, then she might have been able to marry her way in.

She shook her head. She knew the attraction wasn't the sisters-in-law — it was the man himself. And she so wasn't going there.

★　★　★

Mark missed Chrissy like crazy; there was no getting away from it. Which was ridiculous, as she'd only been gone a few hours. He had to admit, though, that without her, the farmhouse was missing a certain vibrancy.

It had taken him a long time to admit it, but as he stood in the barn, paintbrush in hand, he knew without doubt that he was in love. Perhaps he'd always been a bit in love with her. Maybe that was why he hadn't been as easy in her company as his brothers had been.

He'd always been completely aware of how pretty she was, of course he had; it would impossible to ignore. But it obviously went deeper than that.

He cleared away his work things, knowing he wouldn't manage to get any work done tonight. He wanted to phone her, just to hear her voice, but he knew that wouldn't be a good idea.

Instead, he called to Florence and Bob and headed out to the fields. There would still be enough light in the sky to walk for the next hour or so. The two dogs, excited to be going out at this time of night, fell over each other as they ran ahead. And he couldn't help smiling. Though he knew the happy feeling had more to do with being in love than it did with the antics of the dogs.

If only the object of his affection was likely to welcome the sentiments. But he knew he'd best keep a cool head around her.

* * *

Chrissy enjoyed the weekend with the girls. She'd never been one for mixing and joining in, but the McGregor women were lovely and she was glad to be their friend.

She arrived back at work on Monday, keen to tell Mark all about it, even though she suspected he might not be interested. But he surprised her by popping into the office with bacon rolls and tea and propping himself on the edge of her desk.

'Sound like you had a nice time.'

'I did. I've no idea why I was so worried about going.' She smiled. 'I missed you, though.' She felt her eyes widen in surprise. Where had that come from? She glanced up and saw her own shock mirrored on his features. But then the expression faded into a megawatt smile that had her catching her breath.

'Did you, Chrissy?'

She nodded shyly. 'Though I don't suppose I should have told you that.'

He was still smiling, and she suddenly felt very self-conscious.

'Why not?' His smile had faded and there was an intensity in his blue eyes that frightened the living daylights out of her.

'Too much information.' She was breathless; she didn't know why.

'I'm glad you told me.'

The moment was getting way too intimate. The way he was looking at her, it was almost as though he could see into her soul.

She scratched around for something to say that would deflect attention away from what she'd shared. Something that would break the spell and bring them back to what they were — friends. She was supremely aware that her chair was uncomfortably close to where he perched on his desk, his muscular, denim-clad thighs distractingly near. 'How's the painting coming along?'

'Getting there. I hope to be done in time, but I'll be cutting it fine.'

'Can I see what you've done?'

If anything, his smile grew even brighter. 'Of course you can.'

He led the way to the barn, unlocked the door, then pushed it wide to let Chrissy precede him. She reached for the light switch and gasped at the sight that met her: Mark's easel was upturned, paints thrown here and there, and there was no sign of his art.

'What the . . . ?' His harsh tone had her swinging round.

'I take it you didn't leave it like this?'

He shook his head and ran a rough hand through his red hair. 'Someone's been in here since I locked up last night.'

She remembered him saying how much his paintings were worth; about how his insurance company had insisted on the sophisticated security system. And she suddenly felt sick. Someone had stolen Mark's work. And, as the place wasn't properly alarmed, it was probable his insurance company wouldn't pay out.

Mark had gone a worrying shade of pale. Chrissy pushed him gently towards a chair and made him sit. 'Do you have any idea who might have done this?'

He shrugged a large shoulder. 'Some-one with a grudge?'

'A grudge and a key,' she said thought-fully. 'Listen, I'm going to check something out. I'll ring you if I find anything.'

She hated to leave him when he was so obviously upset, but she had to do this before any potential trail got a chance to grow cold.

Her first port of call was her sister's office. Juliet was nothing if not abreast of local gossip.

'Yes, Sam's back in town,' she said, her eyes narrowing as she sensed something sensational. 'Why?'

'Maybe nothing,' Chrissy said. Though he'd promised to get his own back on Mark, and this would be a humdinger of a way to do it. 'But it might be something important.'

Without thinking about the wisdom of such an act, she got into her car and started the engine. Then she followed the track out of the village, up towards the old bothy out at Kinbrae Loch, where Sam lived.

15

Sam's Place

Mark thought he must be very slow on the uptake, but it was only as he heard Chrissy's car drive off that he realised she was leaving the farm. It took a while longer before he realised where she was most probably going.

Panic reached out and grabbed him by the throat. Someone with a grudge and a key: Sam. Mark knew the drivers were aware the wall cabinet in the office housed spare keys for the outbuildings. Chrissy had most probably reached the same conclusion and gone to find him. Stopping only to confirm Sam's address from the staff records, he ran to his car and sped off.

He breathed a sigh of relief as he caught up with Chrissy's car on the road to Kinbrae Loch. Flashing his headlights and hooting to get her attention, he prayed she wouldn't be stubborn enough to keep going. He briefly considered overtaking and blocking her way, but the road was narrow and winding and it wouldn't be safe for either of them.

His relief was overwhelming when she eventually responded to his frantic attempts to stop her and she pulled into a lay-by halfway up the road. Without pausing to catch his breath, he stopped behind her and got out. 'What were you thinking?' he called as she got out of her own car.

She stopped a short distance away and looked up at him, all big green eyes and quizzical expression. He wanted to simultaneously be furious with her for even thinking of confronting Sam on her own, and kiss her senseless for caring so much about his paintings.

As she stood in front of him, the kissing won. And as he took her in his arms and their lips met, he forgot he'd ever been frantic with worry.

'Why are you shouting?' she asked as

they drew apart.

'I'm not.' His arms tightened around her, his protective instincts coming to the fore yet again.

'Well, maybe not now, but you were.'

He sighed and gave in to the urge to lower his lips to hers again. Her hands were suddenly in his hair, pulling him closer; and, for a woman who didn't want romance, she kissed him back with an awful lot of enthusiasm.

'Well?' she asked as they surfaced again, her mouth still the most tempting he'd ever seen. Even if she was now frowning.

'I don't remember,' he said, his hands still on her waist.

'Try.'

He sighed. 'I got some stupid idea into my head that you were going to confront Sam on your own.'

She moved even closer to him and nestled against him, her body language completely at odds with the anger that flashed in her eyes. 'It's my responsibility as acting manager to investigate a crime that was committed while I was in charge.'

He gathered her even closer. The wind had taken on a biting quality; and even now, when she wasn't impressed with him, he wanted to shield her from anything unpleasant.

'Why do you have to make things so difficult?' he asked.

She pulled away, stepped just out of reach, and glared at him. 'Me make things difficult? You're the one who moved into a barn that had no proper security with thousands of pounds' worth of paintings.'

'Point taken,' he said, holding out his hand. 'Come on, we should get going.'

Reluctantly, she reached out and her cool fingers folded around his. He liked that. Even when she was angry she still trusted him enough to take his hand.

He sighed. 'I'm sorry. I can't help worrying when you put yourself in unnecessary danger.'

'Sam wouldn't hurt me.'

He squeezed her hand, hoping she

was right, but suspecting she wasn't. He'd had a nasty look on his face the other day.

'Why take the chance?' he asked. 'You don't have to do everything on your own, Chrissy. It's OK to rely on other people occasionally. Nobody will think you're weak if you do that.'

'But — '

He shook his head to stop her arguing. 'Everyone needs other people sometimes.'

She bit her lip as she thought about what he'd said. And eventually, she nodded. 'OK.'

'And promise me,' he said, 'that in future you'll hang on for me before you go chasing off after criminals. It's not good sense to go off on your own without telling anyone.' He wondered if he'd gone too far and he braced himself for her to tell him exactly that. Instead, she nodded again.

'All right.' And then she smiled and he found it difficult to breathe.

Even though the feminist in her

should be annoyed, Chrissy loved it that Mark was so masterful. Yes, she'd always been fiercely independent; but with Mark around, she'd had a taste of what it might be like to have someone to lean on. And she was frightened by how much she liked leaning on Mark. She wanted him to understand that he could rely on her, too, though.

'OK,' she told him, 'let's get going to see if Sam's in. Shall we take your car, or mine?'

'Yours,' he told her decisively. 'If Sam does have the paintings, we'll need the bigger car to bring them back.'

She drove up in front of the croft where Sam lived and they both got out, Mark rapping neatly at the door.

Sam came to the door looking sheepish.

'Do you have my paintings?' Mark was direct and to the point and Chrissy held her breath as she waited for Sam's response.

Whatever the other man was, at least he didn't try to cover up his crime. He gave a short nod. 'Reckoned you needed taking down a peg or two.'

Mark's smile could have frozen the core of an active volcano. 'You do realise that if I were to press charges you'd likely be looking at a spell in jail?'

The other man shook his head. 'For a first offence? I don't think so.'

'You know how much those paintings are worth,' Mark told him quietly. 'You told me so yourself not so long ago.'

Sam paled, realisation seeming to hit as to how much trouble he might have brought on himself. 'You're not going to call the police, are you? I was only trying to get my own back for the other day. I didn't mean to keep them.' For such a usually obnoxious man, he seemed surprisingly contrite.

There was a long silence. Chrissy held her breath. Then Mark shook his head. 'I won't call the police,' he said, 'as long as you give back what you took. And promise not to come near me or Chrissy again.'

Chrissy looked at him in disbelief.

Why wasn't he calling the police? Why was he letting Sam get away with this?

She waited until they were back in the car, the paintings safely stowed in the back, before she asked.

'If I made it official, the paintings could be tied up for months. They would be evidence.'

'They might be able to use photographs.'

'Possibly. But I have a lot riding on this exhibition. I can't take the risk.'

She nodded. He was right, of course. But she didn't like that Sam had got away with this. He could have ruined months of hard work.

'He won't do anything like that again,' Mark told her, seeming to read her mind. 'He knows that if he does there will be consequences. And the man's already lost his job.'

'His own choice,' Chrissy argued. 'He walked out.'

'Because he knew it was only a matter of time. You said yourself he'd already had a written warning.' She nodded. 'He knows there's no way he'll be allowed back. We don't want to make it impossible for him to find other work.'

She took her eyes off the road just long enough to smile at him. He really was lovely.

They'd arrived back at his car now and she pulled into the lay-by. Before he could get out, she unclipped her seatbelt and leaned towards him. 'The trouble with you, Mark McGregor, is that you're a nice man.'

He flashed his megawatt smile and her heart thumped in her chest. 'Praise, Chrissy?' he said, leaning in towards her.

She could feel his breath, warm on her face; smell the soap and shampoo he'd used that morning. Her breath caught. This kissing business was really getting out of hand, but she couldn't seem to help herself around Mark.

With a soft sigh, she closed the gap between them, and her eyes fluttered closed as their lips met and his arms came around her.

* * *

It seemed like the blink of an eye before Heather and Denny McGregor were due to arrive home from their cruise. Time had flown by — but so much had happened, and Chrissy couldn't imagine why she'd ever been unhappy about Mark moving into the farmhouse. Especially not when she was so upset at the prospect of him moving out.

'I can't believe you'll be leaving,' she said, the sting of tears at the back of her eyes.

'Hey,' he said, pulling her in towards him.

She rested her head on his chest and listened to the reassuring beating of his heart. 'Things won't be the same without you.' She couldn't quite bring herself to tell him that she'd miss him — even if it was the truth.

'You'll be able to get back to normal,' he said.

'Yes.' Though she didn't think she knew what normal was any longer. She certainly couldn't envisage a normal that didn't include Mark. She smiled, but even though she forced her lips to curve, the sentiment behind the gesture was an empty one. She watched Mark pack away his work things with a heavy heart.

'I'll need to book one of the trucks to move everything back home. Will you help me?' he asked. 'I know I could ask one of the drivers . . . '

She put her hand on his arm. 'I might not want you to leave, but if you have to go then I want to be the one to help you, Mark.'

His blue eyes darkened to almost navy, the expression in them inscrutable. She smiled and was glad when he smiled back.

'I'm pleased you said that.'

She frowned. How could he have doubted that she'd be pleased to help? 'That's what friends do,' she told him and, before her eyes, his expression hardened. She watched in fascination as a muscle twitched in his cheek. What had she said wrong?

'And we *are* friends, aren't we?' There was a harshness in his voice that she didn't quite understand.

'Mark, what's the matter? Have I done something to upset you?'

'Nothing that can be helped,' he said as he turned and began to walk away.

The hand that had been on his arm dropped to her side. He was at the door before she realised she couldn't let it end like this. She neatly dashed between him and his escape route.

'What is it, Chrissy?'

'Don't walk away from me, please, Mark.'

'What do you want from me?'

'I want to understand what's going on in your head.'

His eyes narrowed and he seemed to be mulling something over. Then he sighed, and Chrissy felt the impact all the way down to her work boots. 'Oh, Chrissy.'

'What is it?' she asked, lifting her hand towards his arm. But she lost courage before she actually made contact and let it waver there in mid-air.

He spared her the embarrassment of a hovering hand by taking it and holding to his chest, closing his eyes as he did so. She could feel the strong beating of his heart. She wanted, more than anything, to put her arms around him and hold him close, but something stopped her.

Then he opened his eyes — and the intensity of the blue made her breath catch. 'You want to know what's going on in my head?' She nodded. 'It's you. You're in my head.' He paused and she didn't know what to say. Then he sighed. 'And you're in my heart.'

She swallowed painfully, not really knowing where this was leading. 'Mark . . . '

He put the gentle fingers of his free hand to her lips, his other hand still covering hers against his heart. 'Don't, Chrissy — now I've started, I need to finish what I have to say.' She nodded. 'I love you, Chrissy. I think on some level I always have. I don't want to leave you — I don't want to go back to my home without you.'

This was getting out of hand so quickly that she didn't know how to stop him saying the words. And in a way, she didn't want to. Because, even if she didn't quite know how to deal with this, she didn't want him to go home without her, either.

Tell him, a voice urged inside her head — because she'd long since realised that her plans to be independent and alone meant nothing. *Tell him now. Before it's too late.*

But however hard she tried, the words wouldn't come.

He sighed again, and his smile made her want to cry. 'I'll see you at the exhibition tonight,' he told her. 'I'm going to head down there this afternoon, to make sure everything's as it should be.'

Without waiting for her to reply, he let her hand go and walked out.

16

Feels Like Love

Through the cloud of elegance and sparkle that surrounded him, Mark looked towards the door for what had to be the millionth time that night. She wasn't coming — that was pretty obvious. And he only had himself to blame.

Disappointment sank through him right down to his newly polished shoes. He hadn't realised until that moment how much he'd been looking forward to having her at his side tonight. But he'd frightened her off with his careless declaration, just has he'd known he would — which was why he'd kept quiet so long.

He was still glad it was out in the open, though. It had needed to be said. Keeping it to himself had been driving him slowly crazy.

He tried to mingle. He tried to be charming and witty and everything else everyone expected of him. But they were not things that came easily to him at any time, and tonight he was finding them impossible. Without Chrissy here it all seemed an empty waste of time.

'Mark, I like what you've done with the use of colour in this one,' a very lovely young woman with diamonds sparkling at her ears told him.

'Thank you.' His smile was decidedly forced; he hoped she hadn't noticed. The gallery owner had advised him earlier that he needed to be particularly pleasant and outgoing around this woman. Completely unlike himself, really.

The woman smiled at him before wandering off, a glass of Champagne in her hand, and she joined a group nearby. Maybe he was even worse at this mingling lark than he'd thought he was.

He was glancing idly around at the glittering company, feeling completely out of his depth, when he saw her. She'd slipped into the gallery without him noticing — and was standing right inside the door.

She took his breath away.

Her hair was down — straightened until the locks fell in a smooth curtain past her shoulders. And she was wearing a dress: a lime-green shift that fell short of her knees and offered a glimpse of long, slender legs. What was more, she was smiling straight at him, and she didn't take her eyes from his as she covered the short distance between them.

'Hello.' She stood shyly on tiptoes and planted a brief kiss on his lips.

As she did so his hand came up around her waist. He wanted to gather her closer, to kiss her senseless, but he knew this was neither the time nor the place. Instead, he kept his hand around her, holding her close to him.

'I thought you weren't going to turn up,' he whispered into her ear.

'Sorry.' She smiled up at him. 'I couldn't find the gallery.'

She had wondered whether or not

she should just turn around and go home. The fact that she — who prided herself on being a top driver who never got lost — had encountered difficulty in finding this gallery had seemed like a sign. But now she was here, with Mark's hand on her waist giving the unmistakeable signal that they were here together, she was so glad she had persevered.

A glamorous woman wearing the most dazzling earrings swooped down and looked pointedly at Chrissy. 'And you are — ?'

Chrissy didn't like the smug expression on the other woman's face, or the proprietary gleam in her eye as she glanced at Mark. She immediately felt colour rise in her face and she leaned closer towards Mark, laying her claim, and glad of his hand still holding her to him.

She held out her hand to meet the other woman's, and shook it. 'I'm Christina,' she said. 'Mark's girlfriend.'

She felt his fingers tighten almost

imperceptibly on her as a soft chuckle escaped him. She didn't even care that he realised she was jealous.

The other woman's smile could best be described as brittle. 'Well, aren't you the lucky one,' she sneered at Chrissy. Then, after another quick glance at Mark, she disappeared in a cloud of expensive perfume.

Chrissy didn't dare look at Mark. 'Shut up,' she told him pre-emptively.

'Well, Christina.' He ignored her instruction and shivers ran down her spine as he said her name, even though there was amusement in his voice. 'You made short work of that.'

'What you mean?' With face burning, she risked a glance up at him.

He brought his other hand up to her waist and turned her around so that she was facing him. 'I like it when you get possessive over me.'

She wanted to deny it, though she knew it would be useless. He was grinning down at her and soon she found herself smiling back.

'That's better. Chrissy might frown and glower — and it's part of her charm — but Christina shouldn't. Christina is elegant and unruffled.'

She was aware of people milling around, waiting to speak to Mark; she knew he would have to get back to circulating soon. But not yet. 'Who was she, anyway?'

'Someone the gallery owner was hoping might buy the majority of my work this evening.'

It was proof of how lovely he was that he didn't even seem the slightest bit cross Chrissy had chased away someone who might have been his best customer. She wrinkled her nose up at him. 'Sorry.'

He laughed. 'Two apologies in one evening! I need to go out with Christina more often.'

She laughed right along with him, because she liked the sound of going out with him again.

★   ★   ★

Two days later Heather and Denny had returned, and Mark's preparations to leave the farmhouse were complete. He came into the office to see Chrissy before he drove away. 'It seems our time is up,' he joked.

Chrissy was devastated — barely able to breathe, let alone laugh. She managed a tight smile that she suspected must have looked like a grimace, because Mark winced. Without a word, she got up and walked over to him and hugged him briefly, not waiting long enough for him to hug her in return. She didn't dare, because she knew that once she felt his arms around her she'd be reduced to a sobbing heap.

And then he was gone from the office. She heard his car start through the open office window a little while later, then she heard him drive away. But she stayed resolutely in her chair, letting Heather and Denny be the ones to wave him off, knowing she didn't want to watch him go.

Even though Chrissy was delighted

to see her employers back safe and well, she couldn't ignore the ache in her heart. She missed Mark already. And, if history was anything to judge by, he wouldn't be making a habit of popping by the farmhouse any time soon. The fears that had loomed all her life were coming true — she'd allowed herself to fall in love, and now she was losing him to his old life. Though she would be taking his things back in the lorry later in the week; she'd get the chance to see him then.

'Chrissy.' Denny came into the office and sat down in the chair across the desk from her. 'I need to have a word.'

Chrissy experienced a sense of foreboding; it wasn't usual for Denny to be so formal when wanting a chat. Something had to be up.

'Sounds ominous.' Though she smiled, determined to be positive. Mark leaving had hardened her heart; nothing could be as bad as losing him.

'It's the business,' Denny came straight to the point. 'Going away, being able to relax and seeing how well things have run without me, has made me see how I need to take a back seat from now on.'

He sat back and watched her carefully; she guessed he was probably waiting for a violent reaction. Maybe an argument as to why he needed to keep going. But she couldn't bring herself to do it. Without Mark, the future of the business didn't really matter to her any longer. Nothing did. 'Are you thinking of selling up?'

He shook his head. 'No plans to sell up at the moment,' he said. 'But I had a word with Mark before he left. He's agreed to stick around to keep things ticking over while Heather and I decide what we're going to do.'

Chrissy's heart began to hammer. 'Mark's agreed to move back here?' She could barely believe it. Five minutes ago she'd resigned herself to the fact that their relationship had little chance of success, so the discovery that he'd be coming back turned that assumption upside down.

'He's agreed to take a more active part in the business. Not just babysit the building and the animals like he did when we were away.' He paused, probably again expecting a storm of protest, but Chrissy was way too happy to think of anything other than that Mark would be there. With her.

'He'll need your help, mind, Chrissy. He has no business experience at all, other than his hobby of selling those paintings of his.'

Chrissy nodded. 'Of course,' was all she managed to say — even though she knew she should have corrected Denny in his assumption that Mark's paintings were definitely more than a hobby.

Once she was alone, she hummed a tune as she shuffled the invoices that littered her desk. She couldn't focus on a single thing, but this was turning out to be a great day.

It was less than an hour later when her phone rang. She smiled as she saw the name on the display. 'Hello, Mark. When are you coming back?'

'Just as soon as I can. Why, do you miss me?'

'Yes.' No hesitation or evasion, just pure honesty.

'Good.' His voice was low, the tone sending shivers down her spine the way only his voice could. 'I've got a lot more stuff to bring if I'm moving back for the long term.'

'I'll be over with an empty lorry this afternoon.'

★ ★ ★

Chrissy arrived just after lunch; she jumped out of her lorry and ran to where Mark stood waiting for her near his cliff-top house. His heart thumped against his chest as he saw her approach. He held his arms out, picked her up and spun her around before kissing her thoroughly.

Still in his arms, she pulled away from his kiss. 'Will you be happy running the business?' she asked, her beautiful face — only inches from his

— creased into a frown. 'What about your art? Your studio's here — and all this.' She raised her hand to indicate the sea beneath the cliff they were standing on. 'This has been your inspiration.'

He set her back down on her feet, and loved her even more because she was so concerned about what would make him happy.

'I've managed to work in the barn over the past weeks,' he reminded her as they began to walk hand in hand towards the house. 'I'll make time to keep my hand in with the painting, whatever happens with the business.' He paused, brought her hand to his lips, and grazed a kiss on it. 'And I seem to have found a new source of inspiration.'

They went into the house and Mark led the way to his studio. Chrissy spun around to take in the canvases that lined the walls. 'You're going to be wasted at the haulage company.'

He shrugged a broad shoulder. 'What can I do? They need me. Besides . . . ' His big hands circled her waist, and she sighed as he pulled her so she was leaning against him. 'I find I'm suddenly very interested in moving back to the farmhouse.'

She grinned and stood on tiptoe so she could brush her lips against his. 'You could find someone else to run things.'

'Like who? Jack's busy with his family and his own business. And Ryan's not interested in business.'

'Neither are you.'

'I'll have to learn to be.' Not so long ago, he'd thought nothing could have persuaded him to give up his studio and his way of life. But that had been before a certain redhead had taken his heart.

'Or . . . ' There was a gleam in her eye that he couldn't quite read.

'Or what?'

'Or,' she continued, 'we could run things together. I'd do the day-to-day management of things, and you'd only need to be involved with the big decisions. That way you'd have time to carry on with your painting, but still be involved with the company. So you'd keep your parents happy.'

'You'd honestly be OK with that?' He raised an eyebrow. 'Don't you remember how you kicked against the idea of me having anything to do with the place while Mum and Dad were on their cruise?'

She winced at the reminder, and Mark smiled. 'I'd learn to live with it,' she said, her big green eyes looking up at him.

He shook his head. 'I don't know if the family would go for that.'

'Because I'm not a McGregor?'

'Well, they do want to keep the business in the family. That's why they've called me home.'

'There's an easy way to rectify that.' She kept steady eye contact as she waited for his answer.

His heartbeat thumped steadily as the implications of her suggestion sank in. She couldn't possibly mean what it sounded like she meant. 'What way would that be?'

'We could get married,' she said. Then she lifted her small chin and dared him to argue.

'You're not interested in marriage,' he reminded her.

'What if I said that I might have changed my mind?'

'Just to get your hands on the company?'

She shook her head. 'No.' She slipped her arms around his waist and aimed a kiss at his jawbone. 'So I can get my hands on you.'

He smiled; he couldn't help it. And he was tempted to gather her up and kiss her senseless there and then, but something held him back. 'I told you I wasn't going to ask you,' he reminded her. 'I gave you my word. If you want to marry me, you have to propose.'

His breath caught in his throat as she stepped away from him. He'd called her bluff and she was leaving. He wanted to tell her not to go — to reach out the hands that were suddenly empty and hold her close. And so what if she didn't love him as much as he loved her?

But instead of walking out of the door, she reached out and took both his hands in hers. 'Mark McGregor,' she began, looking up at him with her green eyes overly bright, 'I love you more than I ever thought it would be possible to love anyone. I want to share my life with you. Will you marry me? Please?'

Finally, he scooped her up into his arms, and her breath tickled his neck as she laughed.

'I thought you'd never ask.'

Epilogue

'Your mother and I have reached a decision: we're going to make my absence from the business permanent,' Denny admitted to Mark a few weeks later over a cup of tea and chocolate cake in the McGregors' farmhouse kitchen. Surprisingly, he didn't seem very sorry about the fact.

'We're going to spend time enjoying each other's company,' Heather chipped in. 'And taking the holidays we didn't have the time to enjoy when we were both working.'

Mark could see the reasoning behind the argument, and he was grateful his parents had reached the decision without their hands being forced through his father's illness. Thankfully, Denny McGregor was back to almost full fitness.

'Can't say I blame you,' Mark said.

'You've both worked hard over the years.'

'So, as you've been holding the fort, I want you to be the first to know we're planning to sell the haulage business.'

'You can't mean that,' Mark gasped, knowing how much it all meant to his dad.

Denny shrugged a broad shoulder. 'It was my dream, son, not yours. Nor Jack's or Ryan's. I want someone who will take pride in it, be passionate about it.'

Mark shook his head. He couldn't personally see how anyone could be passionate about a fleet of lorries. But luckily, he knew a person who would understand. Slowly, he smiled. She'd be cross, he knew, and angry that he'd meddled and taken it upon himself to spend his money on her. But once she realised all he wanted was for her to be happy, he was sure Chrissy would understand.

'Would you consider selling it to me?' he asked. 'If the rest of the family have no objection, that is.'

Denny's immediate look of delight was quickly reined in. 'You're only saying that because you know how much it means to me that a McGregor runs the place.'

'Partly,' he admitted. Then he grinned and his father's expression relaxed. 'But it's also because I happen to think it would make a perfect wedding present for my future wife.'

We do hope that you have enjoyed reading this large print book.

Did you know that all of our titles are available for purchase?

We publish a wide range of high quality large print books including:
Romances, Mysteries, Classics
General Fiction
Non Fiction and Westerns

Special interest titles available in large print are:
The Little Oxford Dictionary
Music Book, Song Book
Hymn Book, Service Book

Also available from us courtesy of Oxford University Press:
Young Readers' Dictionary
(large print edition)
Young Readers' Thesaurus
(large print edition)

For further information or a free brochure, please contact us at:
Ulverscroft Large Print Books Ltd.,
The Green, Bradgate Road, Anstey,
Leicester, LE7 7FU, England.
Tel: (00 44) **0116 236 4325**
Fax: (00 44) **0116 234 0205**

Other titles in the
Linford Romance Library:

A SONG ON THE JUKEBOX

Pat Posner

Polly has fallen head over heels in love with James Dean-lookalike, skiffle-playing Johnny — whom her mum has judged to be completely unsuitable boyfriend material. When Mum sends Polly to live with Gran in an attempt to split them up, Polly is determined to remain true to Johnny. Will Gran, like Mum, forbid her to see him? And what happened in the past to cause the discord between her grandmother and mother? Polly sets out to discover the truth, and the consequences are surprising . . .

THE TOUCH OF THISTLEDOWN

Rebecca Bennett

When Clare, a recently qualified solicitor, meets Neal on the way to her cousin's wedding in Suffolk, his arrogant views on a woman's place in the profession annoy her. Nevertheless, she finds herself reluctantly becoming very attracted to him, despite her involvement with a married partner in the firm where she works. Suffolk and Neal are never far from her life — or her heart; though when one of her clients makes an unexpected, desperate move, Clare finds she is fighting for her life as well as her future happiness.

LOVE AMONG THE ARTS

Margaret Mounsdon

When Stella Bates arrives at Minster House to take on the position of companion to the injured Lady Pamela Loates, she expects to live quietly in an outbuilding and focus on her photography. Soon, however, she finds herself looking after the two recalcitrant teenagers in the family, and it isn't long before the boorish attitude of Pamela's handsome son Rory softens into affection, and then love. But how long can Stella stay at Minster House, especially when she is being stalked by the sinister Buttonhole Man?